Darcy's Happy Compromise

By Zoe Burton

Darcy's Happy Compromise

Zoe Burton

Published by Zoe Burton

Early drafts of this story were written and posted on Patreon and fan fiction forums in 2022.

ISBN-13: 978-1-953138-24-8

Acknowledgements

First, I thank Jesus Christ, my Savior and Guide. Thank you for giving me the words to write and the inspiration for new stories. I love you!

I owe a debt of thanks to my best writing buddies, Leenie and Rose. Thank you for your friendship and support.

Also, I must thank my patrons at Patreon from the bottom of my heart. Your support tells me that my stories are valuable to you, and it inspires me to continue.

Chapter 1

Friday, October 25, 1811

Lucas Lodge

Fitzwilliam Darcy stepped through the double doors in Sir William Lucas' drawing room and onto the brick veranda between the house and the garden. He had seen Elizabeth Bennet pass through the same doorway a few minutes before, and he was eager to speak to her. With swift but quiet steps, he crossed the paved expanse, entering the gravel path that meandered around the edge of the area. His ears caught the sound of voices, and he stilled, cocking his head to listen, wondering if Elizabeth had come out here to meet someone.

"... strongbox in the study ..."

"What are his ..."

"... tomorrow night."

Darcy's brow creased. The voices were male. He could not make out everything that was said, but what he did hear caused him concern. He hesitated, wondering where Elizabeth had gone and hoping she was not involved in it. Suddenly, a female shriek caught his ear and there she was, charging toward him. A glint of moonlight on steel flashed behind her, and his heart leaped into his throat.

As Elizabeth reached him, Darcy could see a shape behind her, wielding the sword with one hand as it reached for her with the other.

He could not make out the man's features or get a clear view of his clothing – the moon was too dim for that – but he could clearly see that he meant her harm. Darcy called out to her.

"Elizabeth!"

She must have recognized his voice, because she ran straight toward him, just as the man chasing her grabbed hold of the back of her gown. Darcy wrapped her up in his arms and spun her around, covering her with his body. He heard the sound of cloth tearing as he lifted her off her feet. He braced himself, expecting a blow, but it never came. He straightened and looked over his shoulder, keeping Elizabeth in his embrace, but the sword and its owner had disappeared. Darcy's brow creased again as his eyes searched the darkness for them.

Elizabeth gasped and sobbed. "Thank you, Mr. Darcy." She shivered. "I-"

The screech of a female voice startled them both and they jumped apart. "Elizabeth Bennet! And Mr. Darcy!" They looked toward the house to find Elizabeth's aunt, Mrs. Philips, standing at the edge of the veranda just three feet away, her hand over her mouth and her eyes wide. "Your gown ... oh, my! I never thought I would see the day. I must go tell your mother." With that, the lady spun around and ran back to the door and into the house.

"Oh, no." The words escaped Elizabeth on an exhale. "She will make more out of this than it is." She shivered again and stepped back from Darcy's arms, looking over her shoulder. "My gown ... it is ripped. No wonder Aunt Philips thought I was behaving inappropriately." Her eyes closed and she groaned.

It took Darcy no more than half a minute to realize that Elizabeth's aunt believed he and she had been behaving lasciviously. He felt a strange sort of relief at the thought, because he had followed Elizabeth out here to ask her for permission for a courtship. Elizabeth did not know that, however, and he could see signs of distress in her downturned lips and drawn-together eyebrows. He took her small hand in his much larger one.

"I assure you that I will not allow your reputation to suffer for this incident. I will face the results of this willingly and marry you." He let go of her hand and began to remove his coat. "We do not have time to speak of it now, but I am not at all dismayed at the prospect." He paused as he shook the garment out. "Here; put this on. It will cover your gown."

Elizabeth finally spoke, sputtering out a "thank you" and slipping her arms into the sleeves of his tailcoat.

"May I escort you inside?" Darcy held out his elbow to her as he glanced into the house through the open door, where many of the guests had gathered. "I suspect your father will arrive momentarily."

"You may." Elizabeth tucked her hand into

the crook of his arm and sighed. "I do not know how my father will react, but I suspect he will give you no trouble." She stopped, and Darcy followed suit. "I should perhaps feel more upset than I am. I ... I confess to being more numb than anything." She looked up at her companion. "I overheard some men ... the one who chased me ... planning something that sounded nefarious. I could not hear them well, though." She looked over their shoulders into the dark behind them and shivered again. "I have never been so terrified in my life." She turned her face back up to Darcy's. "Thank you for saving me. Who knows what my fate would have been had you not?"

Darcy did not have time to reply, because at that moment, Elizabeth's mother appeared in the doorway.

"Elizabeth Bennet! What are you doing out here in the dark, behaving like a common trollop? Get in this house right now!" Mrs. Bennet pointed with one hand into the house behind her, the other hand fisted on her hip. "Have you no care for your sisters? What you do affects Jane's prospects, and Lydia's. And how am I ever supposed to find someone to take Mary off my hands with a ruined sister? And Kitty, too! Good heavens!" She began to fan herself. "I feel faint. I need my salts!"

Jane Bennet, Elizabeth's elder sister, appeared behind her mother. "Come, Mama. Come in and sit. There is no need to become distressed." She looked at her sister. "If you are through making a spectacle of yourself, Lizzy, Papa is in the other room with Sir William. You should go and present yourself to him before you go home. No one here wants a hussy like you to remain."

Darcy's head drew back, as if slapped, at her cold words. He had noticed on previous occasions the lack of warmth between the siblings, but had not expected anything like this. He looked down at the petite lady at his side. She stood rigidly; nothing else gave him a clue as to her feelings.

"Thank you, Jane." Elizabeth curtseyed. She looked up at Darcy. "Shall we?"

With a nod, Darcy walked forward, her hand still on his arm. Mrs. Bennet and Jane stepped out of the way, and the pair crossed the final steps to the doorway and into the drawing room.

"Are you well, Darcy?" Charles Bingley, one of Darcy's closest friends and the gentleman with whom he was staying for a couple months, was looking at Jane Bennet with a deep crease cutting his forehead in two.

Darcy stopped and glanced back at the pair on the veranda. "I am. I will be happy to do my duty in this instance."

"Good," Bingley murmured. He shook his head and pulled his gaze from the woman outside to his friend. "I am here to assist you in any way possible."

"Thank you. For now, I must speak to Mr. Bennet and then see that Miss Elizabeth gets home safely."

Bingley nodded. "Will you be returning?"

Darcy glanced around, noting the clusters of people talking behind their hands, including his friend's sisters, and the looks of outrage. When two of the neighbors, a woman introduced to him as Mrs. Long and a young lady he thought was her niece, turned their backs, his decision was made. "No, I believe I will return to Netherfield. I have much to consider and many lists to make, and I am tired."

"Then, I will call for the carriage for your use, and you can send it back here for us."

"Thank you, my friend." Darcy gave Bingley a small smile and a nod.

Bingley briefly gripped his friend's shoulder. "Any time." He stepped back.

Darcy moved forward, guiding Elizabeth across the room. Upon reaching the hall, he hesitated.

"They are probably in Sir William's study." Elizabeth gestured to her right.

With a nod, Darcy turned them in that direction. As the sound of chatter from the drawing room faded, he noticed his companion's posture relaxing a bit. He was happy for it. None of this was Elizabeth's fault, and she should not have to suffer as though it was.

When they reached the indicated room seconds later, Darcy knocked and waited for admission.

"Come!"

Darcy pushed down the latch, and the door opened silently. He led Elizabeth into the room.

The gentlemen inside stood hastily, apparently not having expected anyone but servants to disturb their peace. Mr. Bennet, an older gentleman with graying whiskers and a sardonic air about him, looked from Darcy to Elizabeth. He took his daughter's appearance in through a slow perusal.

"Well, Elizabeth, what is this? Why are you dressed in what must be Mr. Darcy's coat?"

Elizabeth's spine stiffened again. "My gown was torn, sir. I had escaped to the garden for some air ... the drawing room was stuffy with all the guests crowded into it and I began to feel restricted in my breathing." She paused a moment. Darcy could hear her take in a deep breath, and then she related the entire tale.

He watched Elizabeth's father as he listened. Bennet's mien clearly displayed his feelings: the quirked brow and the smirk on his lips demonstrated his skepticism as to the veracity of her explanation. Darcy felt his temper rise. He was hard-pressed to remain silent, but so far, the matter resided between father and daughter.

"Your aunt was in here, decrying your ruin." He flicked a hand. "I sent her off with a bug in her ear, but here you are, standing before me just as she described." He tilted his head. "Well, she did not mention the gentleman's garment. She did say your dress was damaged, though." He turned to Darcy. "What have you to say?"

"Miss Elizabeth has told you the truth. I was witness to almost the entire thing. Nothing untoward happened between us, not in the manner in which Mrs. Philips has alluded to. However, based on the whispers and actions of the other guests, it appears the local society, or what of it is in attendance, believes her words. I have already assured your daughter that I will do the right thing and marry her."

Bennet snorted softly. "Then what do you need me for?" He waved them away and resumed his seat. "Be off with you."

Darcy glanced at Elizabeth then turned his attention back to her father. "Are you granting your permission for us to marry, then?"

"Yes, yes. By all means, marry her."

Darcy was aghast at the utter lack of care Mr. Bennet was displaying. "I will go tomorrow and apply for a common license. We will have to wait at least a se'ennight to marry. When shall I come to see you to work out the marriage settlement?"

Bennet's attention was already focused on his next move on the chess board. He looked up and scowled. "What?"

"Miss Elizabeth's settlement. We must draft it."

"Oh, yes." He turned his scowl in Elizabeth's direction. "Tomorrow, I suppose. Best to get it over with quickly. My brother Philips is my solicitor. He can draw up the final papers." He turned back to the game.

Darcy could see clearly that he and Elizabeth had been dismissed. He bowed to Bennet, and to Sir William, who bowed in return, looking almost embarrassed at his friend's behavior. Then, he turned his now-betrothed toward the door and into the hall.

The pair walked in the direction of the front door, going past the drawing room and hearing the noise of the guests as they listened to one of the ladies playing the pianoforte. When they got to the entry hall, Darcy asked for their wraps.

"The carriage is out front, sir." The Lucas' male servant bowed.

Darcy nodded and took Elizabeth's arm, guiding her out the door and down the steps. He handed her into the carriage, climbed in behind her, and knocked on the ceiling. The equipage lurched into motion.

"I am sorry, sir. I am positively humiliated at my father's reaction to our situation." Elizabeth sighed. "I should have expected it, I suppose. We interrupted his game. He hates to be interrupted."

Darcy was quiet for a moment as he gathered his thoughts. "I cannot claim to understand his actions, or his feelings, for that matter. I cannot imagine being so unconcerned

13

about those under my care." He thought about his sister, left broken-hearted by a cad just three months ago at the age of fifteen. He ground his teeth as the remembered feelings of rage rose up in him again. He breathed through his nose as he pushed the emotions down. When he was calm again, he spoke.

"I promise you to never become angry that you have interrupted me, and I further vow that I will protect you to the best of my ability from this day forward. My hands will be tied to a point until we marry, but I consider you to be my wife as of this moment, and one of my duties as a husband is protection." He fell silent. "I am sorry you were threatened in such a manner ... treated so infamously. Whoever the culprit was, he was not a gentleman. He could not have been, for no gentleman who warrants the name would do as that man did. I will ask around and see if I can discover his identity. He should be turned in to the magistrate and dealt with."

Elizabeth was silent for a long moment. "Thank you," she finally replied. "I do not know what to say." She paused for another long moment. "You are taking this very well. It is not what I expected."

"To be honest, I followed you into the garden to ask you for a courtship. You see, I decided days ago that you fit my requirements for a wife. I learned when we danced at the assembly that you are intelligent and well-read. I made a point of conversing with you and listening to your conversations with others over the last few days and discovered that our tastes in many things are similar. Our opinions in the most important of matters are one. We are, I believe, well-suited to one another."

Again, Elizabeth was silent for a few minutes. Then, she replied with a hint of confusion in her voice. "You are a wealthy man. Surely you are aware of the rumors that floated through the assembly hall that you have ten thousand a year. Have you perhaps not heard that I have nothing? My dowry is so small as to be non-existent. You could do far better than me ... are there no ladies in your own circle that would do?"

Darcy shook his head, though he knew she could not see him in the dark. "No, there are not. I decided on the ride out here to Hertfordshire that I would marry a country girl, if I could find one to suit." He paused. "I have found myself increasingly disenchanted with the ladies of high society. I would rather have a wife who will be a companion and a complement to me than one who is merely an adornment." He shrugged. "It is not what is expected of me by some of my family members, but I am my own master. I could not bear to live the rest of my life essentially alone. So, no, there are no ladies in my own circle that would do."

Elizabeth was quiet for a long moment. "I

see." Darcy heard her sigh. "Well, then, I suppose I should confess that I have also wished to marry a man who would be a companion to me and I to him. It bodes well for our union that we have a common goal, does it not?"

"Indeed, it does." Darcy was quite pleased with Elizabeth's declaration. He felt the carriage slow and glanced out the window. "I believe we have arrived at Longbourn."

"Yes."

Darcy recognized weariness in her voice.

When the equipage stopped and the groom had opened the door, Darcy stepped out and turned to hand his betrothed down. He tucked her fingers under his arm and escorted her to the home's entrance. He turned to face her.

"I will be here tomorrow afternoon. I must spend time with your father, but I should like to speak to you. Perhaps we can meander through the garden for a while?"

In the dim light, he could see Elizabeth's lips lift in a small smile.

"That would be lovely. I look forward to it." She curtseyed. "Good night, Mr. Darcy."

Darcy bowed. "Good night, Miss Elizabeth." He watched her enter the home and when the door had shut behind her, turned and took the few steps to the carriage. A quarter hour later, he was descending from it again, this time in front of Netherfield.

Chapter 2

Darcy had just completed his evening ablutions when he heard a noise in the hall that indicated his host's return. Hearing a knock on his chamber door, he stood from the chair by the fire, set his book on the small table beside it, and tightened the belt on his dressing gown. His valet, Mr. Smith, opened the door and, after a few words from the person on the other side, allowed Bingley to enter.

"Are you well, Darcy? I am glad I did not find you abed already."

Darcy gestured toward the other chair that was placed in front of the fireplace and on the other side of the table. "I was going to read for a while first. Would you like a glass of port?" Upon hearing his friend's positive reply, he turned to Smith. "Bring another glass." He then settled back into his seat. "What happened after we left?"

Bingley shook his head. "The party went on as before, but talk never ceased. In every quiet moment between songs, Mrs. Bennet could be heard declaring to all and sundry how awful Miss Elizabeth is and how none of her other daughters would ever behave in such a wild manner." He fell silent as Smith re-entered the room, glass in hand.

Darcy accepted the vessel from his valet

and poured some of the port from the carafe on the table into it. He handed it to Bingley.

"How did the neighbors react?"

Bingley took a sip of his drink and rested his hand, holding the glass, on the arm of the chair. "I think they were titillated. Most of them, anyway. A few made noises about not believing Miss Elizabeth capable of such a thing. They were less certain of you, of course. You are new to the area and essentially unknown. You are considered to be handsome and amiable.

"I heard mention of the dance the two of you shared at the assembly. Some people seemed to suspect you had formed an attachment or something, because she is the only person you danced with, other than my sisters. I was approached to give my opinion, but I declined." He lifted his shoulders and lowered them. "I have no information about it."

Darcy decided not to comment on that statement, instead asking, "Did they treat the Bennets any differently than before?"

Bingley tilted his head and looked away for a moment. Then, he brought his gaze back to his friend. "No, not really. I got the impression that nothing any Bennet does is surprising. I did hear some astonishment at Miss Elizabeth being at the center of it. It seems she is usually much better-behaved than certain other members of the family." He fell silent for a few seconds. "If you are asking about her reputation, tongues were wagging and heads shaking. I do not know how the neighbors will treat her in the future, but the general consensus was that the apple does not fall far from the tree, no matter how well-taught it is."

Darcy pressed his lips into a thin line. "I see." He sighed. "To answer your question, I would not say I have formed an attachment to Miss Elizabeth, but I had already decided to request a courtship from her."

Bingley's brows rose. "You had?"

"I had." Darcy took another sip of his port.

"My sister will be disappointed, I think. Though, now that I consider it, she may not." Bingley chuckled. "After you spoke to her so sharply last month, she seemed to think a baron to be more acceptable than a mere gentleman."

Darcy lifted his glass in a mock toast. "To Baron Edgewood. I wish Sir Stephen every happiness. If I had known all these years that the way to get Caroline to leave me be was to embarrass her, I would have done it much sooner."

Bingley laughed. "She has been rather persistent, has she not?"

"Persistent is not the word for it. I am exceedingly pleased to hear of her new attachment."

Bingley shrugged again. "I suspect he needs her dowry. But, she will be his problem, once he proposes and they marry." He swirled his glass, watching the liquid spin around the sides. "She told me recently that she objected to me forming an attachment with Miss Bennet. After the behavior I witnessed tonight, I agree with her. Miss Bennet is not the woman for me. It is a shame that beauty such as hers covers up a cold heart."

Darcy watched his friend, tilting his head and creasing his brow. "Behavior?"

"Did you not notice?" Bingley looked up at Darcy, brows lifted. "She called her sister a hussy to her face, and then, when she got back to the drawing room, she referred to her in the same manner to everyone else. It was not sisterly at all." He shuddered. "I am treated that way by my own sisters. I do not want to be tied to a wife who behaves so toward me."

"No, I suppose not." Darcy drained his glass, setting it on the table. "Do you have any other information to impart?"

Bingley shook his head. "No." He did as his friend had and then stood when Darcy did. "Shall we ride in the morning?"

"I plan to, yes. I have to visit the rector in the afternoon to purchase a license and then call afterwards at Longbourn to speak to Mr. Bennet about Elizabeth's settlement. I had planned to go out early."

Bingley nodded. "I will tell my valet to get me up just before dawn, then. Good night." He turned and strode to the door, but looked back before he opened it. "I am proud to be called your friend, you know. You handled a difficult situation with grace and aplomb. It was very well done."

One side of Darcy's mouth lifted in a half-grin. "Thank you."

With that, Bingley nodded and left, and Darcy was once again alone with his thoughts. He turned to the bed, untied and removed the dressing gown, and climbed onto the mattress. As he pulled the covers up and settled down under them, he chuckled. "Only you, Bingley." He turned his mind then to Elizabeth and how he wanted her settlement worded. He drifted off to sleep, his mind full of his future wife.

~~~***~~~

The next morning proceeded exactly to Darcy's plans. He and his friend took a long ride across the fields and around the estate. He broke his fast, and then rode toward Longbourn's church. The rector, who had been in attendance at Lucas Lodge the night before, was friendly and obliging, and within a half-hour he was getting back into the saddle, a common license in his hand. The distance from the church to the manor house was short, so moments later, he was dismounting and handing his reins to a groom.

Darcy took the shallow set of steps two at a time and knocked on the door.

He handed the servant his card and stepped inside when she invited him to. "I am here to see Mr. Bennet."

21

"If you wait here, sir, I will see if the master is available." The woman, whom Darcy supposed was the housekeeper based on her clothing and the ring of keys hung around her waist, curtseyed and turned, hurrying toward the back of the house, to the right of the staircase.

While he waited, Darcy took in his surroundings. Longbourn's entry hall was smaller than Pemberley's but slightly larger than that of his house in London. It was tastefully decorated and clean. It was clear the house was old; wear was visible on the wood floor in spots, and the carpet that lined the center of the hall had minor spots of wear on the edges in front of the doorways. Despite these small flaws, the home was well-maintained and did not appear shabby in the least. On one wall was a modest fireplace. Opposite that, there were a few portraits, he assumed of Bennet ancestors. The housekeeper's return brought his attention back to his task.

"If you will follow me, sir." The servant curtseyed again and beckoned him to accompany her.

Near the back of the house, the woman led him to a door, upon which she knocked. Darcy heard a voice bid her to enter. She opened the panel, stepped inside, and announced him.

"Mr. Darcy."

The servant curtseyed again, then moved out of the way so Darcy could enter. She silently exited behind him and closed the door.

Mr. Bennet stood behind his desk, his lips turned down. "Mr. Darcy." He bowed. When he had straightened, he gestured toward a chair in front of him. "Have a seat. My brother Philips should be joining us shortly."

"I am happy to wait." Darcy bowed in return and did as requested. "I have given Miss Elizabeth's settlement much thought over the course of the last several hours." He reached into his pocket. "Here you will find a statement of credit from my banker and an outline of what I wish to give her. I used my recollection of my mother's marriage articles as a guide."

Bennet accepted the papers Darcy held out to him and untied the string holding them together. He examined both before laying them on the desk. "You intend to be generous with her."

Darcy studied Elizabeth's father's mien for a clue as to his feelings on the matter. Seeing nothing, he shrugged. "It is an amount commensurate with what she should receive as Mrs. Darcy. Her station will rise upon our union and she must have the funds available to her to move about comfortably among the members of her new society."

"She has nothing, you know." Bennet smirked. "So this will all be one-sided on your part."

Darcy paused. He already knew Elizabeth's portion was small; that was not a surprise. He wondered at her father's apparent joy in it, though. "That is unfortunate," he said. "However, it is not a problem. As you see ..." He tipped his head toward the letters on the desk. "My income is high enough to make up for it." He looked Bennet in the eye. "I should tell you that I had intended to ask your daughter for a courtship last night even before her aunt misinterpreted what she saw. Her portion or lack thereof means nothing to me."

Bennet eyed Darcy for a long moment before snorting and sitting back in his seat. "I do not know why you would want her. She is just as silly as the rest of the females in this family. I only educated her to shut her up and get her out of my library." Before he could continue, someone knocked on the door. "Come," he called, irritation clear in his tone.

"Mr. Philips is here, sir."

"Send him in, Hill."

The housekeeper followed the same proccdures she had with Darcy.

Two minutes later, Elizabeth's uncle had joined the gentlemen in the book room. Bennet poured drinks for the three of them, and they set to work.

An hour after that, Darcy stood, tucking his papers back into the inside pocket of his coat. "Thank you, Mr. Philips, for your time and attention to this matter."

Philips bowed. "I am happy to be of service. I will write up the clean copy as soon as I get to my office and then set my clerk to making duplicates for you and my brother. I will have them ready for your signature by Friday." He turned to his brother-in-law. "Shall we again make use of your room for that?"

Bennet, already seated, waved his hand toward them. "I suppose we must. If you will leave me to my library once more, I would be appreciative." He picked up a book that had lain on the desk the entire time they had worked.

Darcy pressed his lips together, but gave his future father-in-law a shallow bow, did the same to Philips, and then turned on his heel and exited the room without a word. Upon reaching the hallway, he breathed in through his nose and exhaled, mentally shaking off the strain of being polite to someone whose behavior appalled him.

Mrs. Hill appeared at his side. "Miss Elizabeth is in the front drawing room, sir. If you will follow me?"

Again, Darcy found himself trailing along behind the short, round, older woman and being announced, this time to a room full of females, who stood at his entrance. He looked at each face until he found the one he wished to see. He smiled at her.

"Mr. Darcy."

Mrs. Bennet drew his attention. He looked to see her curtsey elegantly.

"Welcome to Longbourn."

Darcy bowed. "Thank you. I am happy to be here."

"I assume your presence means you are taking Lizzy off my hands?" The matron cocked her head as she spoke, looking for all the world like a bird.

Darcy's already-stretched patience was strained further by his hostess' poorly worded question. He paused and gathered himself before he spoke. "I am marrying Miss Elizabeth, yes. I purchased a license today. We may marry any time after Friday next, as long as we do not wait more than ninety days."

Mrs. Bennet's brows rose as her hands fluttered in front of her. "Oh, well, given the circumstances, it will not do to wait as long as that. You will marry the following Saturday. That is a fortnight from today."

Darcy looked to see what Elizabeth's opinion might be and found that she was looking at her hands. A crease appeared between his brows as he contemplated what that might mean. Slowly, he replied to her mother as a desire to protect his betrothed rose within him.

"Two weeks from today is perfect. I see no reason to wait. Miss Elizabeth is everything lovely, and I am eager to make her my bride." He was gratified to see the blush on her cheeks when she quickly raised her head to look at him.

"Good." Mrs. Bennet turned back to the table near the window at which she had apparently been sitting. "I have been drawing up plans for the ceremony and a breakfast after it. She may have behaved in a very poor manner, but any daughter of mine that marries will be feted."

"Mama, I told you, Mr. Darcy did not tear my gown. He saved me from the man who did."

"If you insist, Lizzy." The matron waved her second daughter away. "Sit down. You are tearing my nerves to pieces, standing about the way you are."

Darcy clenched his jaw. He could feel his face flush as he worked to rein in his growing anger. The touch of a hand on his arm caught his attention. He looked down to see Elizabeth's eyes pleading with him. He gave her a nod and followed her to a settee a few feet away. He sat beside her, taking deep breaths in through his nose and out his mouth, willing himself to relax.

Mrs. Bennet drew his attention again. "Did Mr. Bingley not accompany you today, Mr. Darcy? I hope everything is well with him. Did he say if he would visit later in the afternoon?"

Darcy looked once more at Elizabeth, sitting at his side, hands clenched in her lap and head lowered, before he answered. "He did not come with me. He had some business to take care of today, but he did not share with me what it was, nor did he indicate his plans for the remainder of the day."

"Oh!" Mrs. Bennet seemed taken aback. "I am surprised. He was so taken with my Jane." She shrugged. "Oh, well. I am certain he will return another day. If you were not already betrothed to Lizzy, I would encourage you to consider Jane." She tilted her head, examining the pair on the settee. "Perhaps I should, anyway. We can always send Lizzy away so as not to ruin her sisters' chances of making good matches."

Darcy's barely-held-in-check anger was beginning to fray further. He looked at Elizabeth again. Her posture had become stiff; he could see that she had looked up and was staring in her mother's direction with an expression that could only be described as loathing. He stood.

"I feel a very great need for some fresh air." He turned slightly toward his betrothed. When he spoke to her, he chose to soften his tone. "Would you accompany me to the gardens? I thought we might take a walk."

When Elizabeth nodded her consent, he held out his hand to her, wrapping his fingers around hers as she rose.

Mrs. Bennet frowned and Darcy thought she might deny them permission to leave the room, but she did not. "Jane," she said, "would you like to accompany your sister on a walk?"

Jane looked up from the needlework she had been diligently applying herself to once she realized Bingley had not accompanied his friend. "No, Mama. I would rather remain indoors in comfort."

"Then you shall." The matron smiled indulgently at her eldest daughter. "I see no reason for a fallen child to have any chaperone at all." She looked at Darcy and Elizabeth. "You may walk out alone. I am not chaperoning you and I will not ask any of my other daughters to do so."

Darcy clenched his jaw again, determined not to say anything to further distress his betrothed.

"I will go with you." Mary, Elizabeth's next younger sister, set aside her book and stood. "Appearances must be preserved, regardless of how your match was made."

Darcy noted the small smile Mary gave her sister and counted it in her favor.

"Thank you, Mary. We would welcome your presence. Would we not, sir?" Elizabeth looked up at him, one brow arched.

"We would, indeed." Darcy bowed to Mary and to the rest of the Bennet ladies and led Elizabeth out of the room, her sister trailing behind.

Chapter 3

It only took a few minutes for the three to don their outerwear and leave the house. Darcy was happy to see Mary following a few feet behind, because it left him and Elizabeth free to speak without concern for who would hear.

"Thank you for suggesting this, sir." Elizabeth gestured to the path ahead of them. "It has been a trying morning and exercise always helps me clear my mind of excess emotions."

Darcy lifted his brows at her words. "I am glad I could assist you." He tilted his head and looked down at her. "What has happened?"

"Well, my mother, for one thing. I am certain you noticed her manner toward me today."

"I did." Darcy listened carefully as he kept his eyes on the path before him.

"It has gotten worse over the course of the day." She sighed. "I have tried and tried to tell her what really happened last night, but she refuses to hear it."

Darcy was not certain how he should reply. "I am sorry." He hesitated. "I do not know if it helps, but we do marry in only a fortnight. Can you bear her that long?" He paused as a thought entered his mind. "Perhaps, if she is too much, we may wed earlier. We must wait until Saturday next, at least, but I am willing to move the ceremony up a week if it is necessary."

Elizabeth smiled up at him, making his heart swell with a feeling he could not name.

"Thank you. I will do my best to bear her for as long as I can. Knowing there is an end date will help, as will having the ability to marry earlier, should it become necessary."

"Your happiness and safety are my first concern, always." Looking into her upturned face, he placed his free hand over hers where it rested on his arm. "You say the word, and I will make it happen." He felt a smile slowly spreading over his countenance in answer to hers. "Tell me about the rest of your morning. Are you an early riser, or have you only been out of bed for a short time today?"

Elizabeth's lips suddenly turned down. Darcy's did the same, and his brows drew together as she gazed ahead of her.

"I am an early riser. I was up at dawn for a walk to my favorite place." She fell silent.

Darcy chewed his lip for a long moment as he waited for her to continue. When she did not, he gave in to a strong urge to hear what happened. "That sounds delightful. Where is this place?"

Elizabeth glanced up at him. "Oakham Mount. It is not really a mountain; it is more like a rise ... a high point in the area. Though, it does drop off steeply on one side. There is a large exposed boulder at the top where I like to sit. I can see all of Longbourn from there."

"Perhaps we can walk there one day in the

coming week." Darcy watched her closely.

Elizabeth shrugged. "I would like that. It is not terribly arduous, so I would not have to worry about you becoming winded or anything, I should think." She flashed him a grin that made him smile, but then frowned once more.

"I have to wonder why, if it is your favorite place to walk to, you have such an unhappy look on your face when you tell me about it. Perhaps you do not wish to share it with me?"

Elizabeth looked up at him again, eyes wide. "Not at all! It is important, I think, for us to visit places that have meaning for each other. I will be happy to show it to you." She paused. "My hesitation stems from something else. Something that happened while I was out today." She stopped speaking once more and bit her lip.

Darcy was momentarily distracted at the sight of his betrothed's lip between her even, white teeth. He mentally shook himself, wondering at his behavior. "Will you tell me about it?"

Elizabeth sighed. She gnawed her lip for another few seconds, but then opened her mouth and began to speak.

"Everything was as it always is when I walked up the hill. When I came down, however ..." She hesitated, and Darcy thought she might be searching for words. "I got about halfway down. From that point, one can see the intersection of the roads to Meryton, Lucas Lodge, and Stoke at the point where

Longbourn's drive begins. The woods stop just there, and the estate his bordered, as you know, by a low stone fence. Beyond that fence is the road." She looked up at him.

Darcy nodded, encouraging her to continue.

She looked ahead again. "Rarely is anyone on that lane, and no one ever lingers at the intersection; and yet, when I came out of the trees, there was a militia officer standing between the fence and the road, watching me." She shuddered. "At first, I stopped in surprise. I had not expected anyone to be there."

Darcy saw her lick her bottom lip, a furrow formed between her brows and wrinkles in her forehead. He wanted to interrupt but knew he needed to allow her to tell her story completely.

"I was uncomfortable and I cannot tell you why, at least, not why I was immediately so. As you may have noticed, I do not have a problem speaking to people. I enjoy making conversation with everyone I see and am happy to at least wave at the neighbors if I do see them on the road. There was just something about the soldier, about his stance, that I did not like. I continued down the path until I could see his features more clearly, and that was when I truly became alarmed. He glared at me rather fiercely. He uncrossed his arms – for that was how he had been standing, with his arms crossed in front of him – and rested his hand on the hilt of his sword." She shuddered again. "I did not speak. I gave him a shallow curtsey and a nod and continued on."

Once again, Darcy felt the need to interrupt. This time, he did.

"Have you spoken of this to your father?"

"Not yet. I had not been back long when you arrived, and he was in the library with you and Uncle for quite a while." She sighed. "I will, though. I will have to choose my time." She turned her head toward the side, and Darcy could not see her expression.

"Do you know which officer it was?" He watched her closely.

"Yes. I think so, anyway." She glanced up at him and sighed. "I believe it was Mr. Denny."

"Mr. Denny." Darcy fell into thought, trying to place the man. "Was he not one of the gentlemen flirting with your youngest sisters last night?"

Elizabeth nodded. "Yes, he was."

After further contemplation, during which he and his betrothed walked in silence, Darcy shared his ruminations. "I must ask Bingley if the officers returned to the party once we left, and if so, which ones did."

Elizabeth's brows rose as she glanced at him. "Returned to the party?"

"Yes." Darcy stopped as a thought struck him. "Elizabeth, do you know who it was who chased you down?"

"No. I heard voices and stepped back to leave them alone when I tripped over a bench at the edge of the path. I cried out and heard the bushes rustle, so I turned and ran."

Darcy's fingers, which still lay over Elizabeth's, gripped her. "Elizabeth, it was an officer chasing you. He brandished a sword. If I had not been there ..." He shuddered. "I cannot bear to think of it."

Elizabeth's eyes had gone wide. Her mouth hung open. She began to speak but stopped herself, then repeated her actions once more. Finally, she swallowed. "A sword? It was an officer who chased me?"

Darcy nodded. "Yes, it was."

"I could have been killed!" Her eyes closed. "Thank you, sir," she whispered when she opened them again. She drew in a shaky breath. "You saved more than my reputation; you saved my life!"

Darcy was uncomfortable with her words, for a couple reasons. First, he had only done what anyone would do, and second, while her gratitude was understandable and appreciated, he did not wish for that sort of attention to be directed at him. He was a quiet man and wished to continue in that manner. He tried to tell her so as gently as possible.

"It was nothing any other gentleman would not have done. Please, say nothing else about it." He shifted on his feet, feeling his cravat tighten. He looked around before turning his focus back to Elizabeth. "We have nearly completed our circuit of the gardens. I would ask you to curtail your walks, and to tell your father what happened."

Elizabeth stood straighter, lifting her chin and removing her hands from his. "I will tell Papa, but I will not stop walking. I cannot maintain my sanity for long without a daily ramble and I will not attempt to do so. One of the things you should, perhaps, learn about me sooner rather than later is that I do not like being ordered about." She crossed her arms over her chest.

Darcy was silent for a long moment, his startled and concerned gaze caught up in her defiant one. He considered arguing. After all, they were to be married and he would then be in charge of her. A few months ago, before Georgiana's folly and his subsequent disgust of society's ladies, he would have. However, one of the things he had noticed about Elizabeth that he had found particularly attractive was her independence. She knew her own mind and was unafraid when it came to expressing her opinions and desires. He could not bear to squash that. He did not wish to. So, because he wanted her to remain safe, he attempted to negotiate with her.

"Very well. You are not yet my wife in reality, despite my feelings in the matter. I beg of you, though, to do as I ask. If that is not feasible, please take someone with you. Do you have a footman or groom who might be suitable? Or a maid?" He waved a hand to his left, where Mary stood six feet or so away, head cocked and clearly listening in. "Or Miss Mary, if she were willing, might do."

Darcy watched the emotions crossing Elizabeth's face. She pressed her lips into a thin line, but then dropped her arms and acquiesced.

"Very well, Mr. Darcy. I will take someone with me when I walk." She raised a hand, index finger pointing to the sky. "But, I *will* walk. Do not mistake me in this."

Breathing a sigh of relief, Darcy tipped his head. "I will not. Thank you."

"Thank *you*," she replied. "I apologize if I was too sharp with you. I wish to be your companion, not your servant." She slipped her hand under the crook of his elbow when he offered it.

Darcy shook his head, relieved that they were once again on solid ground, so to speak. "I do not wish you to be a servant to me. It is my duty to protect and care for you and I take my duties very seriously. I am used to giving orders and having them obeyed, but you are not my steward or housekeeper. You are to be my wife. I must become accustomed to speaking to you before I make decisions that affect you." He paused. "I am not one to think the way my elders did, that as the man of the house, I am some sort of god. I make mistakes, and I wish for a partner in life to keep me in check." He smirked. "I think you will do just fine."

Elizabeth laughed, and Darcy joined her.

They continued the last few feet of the path in silence and were soon back in the house.

Darcy remained for another quarter hour. After promising Elizabeth that he would escort her to church the next morning, he made his farewells and returned to Netherfield.

Chapter 4

The next morning, Darcy took his usual early morning ride. Bingley had not yet arisen and so did not join him, but he was not surprised. The pair of them, along with Bingley's brother-in-law, Mr. Hurst, had indulged after dinner a little more heavily in the port than was their wont. *Well,* he thought, *Bingley and I overindulged. For Hurst, it is a daily occurrence.* He snorted to himself, because he knew shaking his head would cause him more harm than the situation currently warranted. After riding a great deal less vigorously than usual, he returned to the house to change his attire and break his fast. Bingley was in the breakfast room when he arrived, sipping a steaming cup of coffee.

"Good morning. Did you ride?" Bingley's voice was cheerful, but lacked his usual high spirits.

"I did." Darcy headed to the sideboard and began to heap eggs and ham onto his plate, as well as kippers and anything else meat- or fish-like he could find. He knew from his admittedly rare previous experiences with over-indulgence that such things would reduce the pounding in his head. He returned to the table, setting the plate down and nodding to the footman who offered to pour him coffee. Darcy saw his friend eyeing his plate and looking slightly green.

"I do not know how you could, or how you will, possibly consume all that. It is positively nauseating." Bingley shuddered.

"I did not gallop, trust me. I held Apollo to a trot or a walk at all times." He shoved a forkful of eggs into his mouth, chewed and swallowed, then took a sip of coffee. "As for my meal, it will ease my aching head in a short while. You should try it." Darcy smirked to see his friend shiver again.

"Thank you, no. Maybe later." Bingley drank some more coffee. "You are going to church with the Bennets?"

"I am. I am picking Elizabeth up a quarter hour before service begins." He looked out the window, squinting up at the sky. "Though, it is just as quick to walk from the manor house to the church as long as it does not rain." He turned his attention back to his plate.

"Caroline wishes to attend services in Meryton, so that is where we will go." Bingley reached into the pocket of his tail coat. "She mentioned some parties to be held this week. She listed the ones she had accepted for us. She assumes you will wish to attend."

Darcy nodded and accepted the paper. When he could, he replied, "I will check with Elizabeth and let you know."

Bingley nodded and then winced. "Excellent. I will tell my sister."

Darcy nodded, and then the pair engaged in further conversation while he finished eating.

~~~***~~~

Darcy arrived at Longbourn closer to a half-hour before services than a quarter-hour. Though Elizabeth was dressed and down-stairs, the rest of the family was not. He could hear a commotion above his head that told him they were still getting ready to go.

"Good morning, Mr. Darcy." Elizabeth curt-seyed. "You are early. Would you like some-thing to eat?"

Though he was still full from his meal at Netherfield, he thought he spied one of his fa-vorite pastries on the sideboard. He bowed and then replied, "I think I will. Thank you." He moved toward the wall where the meal was laid out. "How are you this morning?"

"I am well. I have had my walk and broken my fast and was able to avail myself of the maid before anyone else was out of bed." Elizabeth seated herself and flashed him a grin.

Darcy chuckled at the triumph he detected in her smile. "Excellent." He chose a seat be-side her. "Did you take someone with you?"

Elizabeth's brow rose as she sipped her tea. Darcy felt an unexpected surge of affection overtake his senses at the sight.

"I did." She set the cup down and looked at him. "I took one of the stable boys. He enjoys walking as much as I do and was happy to be my escort and guard for the morning."

"Excellent. Thank you."

Elizabeth said nothing else, instead smiling at him and drinking her tea. The pair fell silent while Darcy finished his pastry and coffee. A noise at the top of the stairs made them both look toward the door. Elizabeth rose. "My sisters will be down momentarily. Would you like to wander the gardens with me again for a few minutes?"

Darcy wiped his mouth on his napkin and dropped it next to his plate as he stood. "I would." He held his elbow out to her. When she tucked her small hand under it, he escorted her into the entry hall. A few minutes later, they were dressed in their outerwear and exiting the house to the sound of Kitty and Lydia arguing as they descended the staircase.

Elizabeth breathed a huge sigh when the door closed behind them. "Thank you for agreeing to this. I know we must leave in just a few minutes, but they are so noisy in the mornings that it quite gives me a bad head."

Darcy chuckled. "I am happy to be of service." He paused. "I am surprised at your parents. I would have expected one of them to reprimand the girls for such behavior."

Elizabeth frowned and lifted her shoulders. "Papa is probably already locked in his book room, and Mama only indulges them. Well, she indulges Lydia. Kitty simply does not get noticed and so gets away with whatever Lydia leads her into."

"I see." Darcy was quiet for a couple

minutes before he spoke again. "Are Miss Lydia and Miss Kitty close, then?"

"I would not call them close. They are just as likely to belittle each other as get along. My parents ..." She hesitated. "Well, my parents really did not raise us to be friends with each other. I have observed that Jane and Lydia are favored, Jane for her beauty and Lydia for her liveliness. At least, Mama favors them. I am uncertain Papa likes any of us. I seem to bear the brunt of my mother's anger." She smirked as she turned her eyes up at him. "I am not the boy she expected, you see, and I was always after her to teach me things. She sent me to my father and he hired tutors and masters and gave me books, probably to shut me up and remove me from his library. Mama resents my education, I think. She believes I am unmarriageable and has long bemoaned the fact that she will have to support me when Papa dies and she is 'thrown into the hedgerows'."

Darcy was taken aback by this information. "Will she be thrown out when Mr. Bennet passes?"

Elizabeth shrugged. "I do not know, but there is a small house about halfway to the back boundary of the estate that I assume is hers as part of her settlement. I remember my grandmother living there before she died."

Darcy nodded. "Perhaps she does not know, either. If your father has not spoken of it, he may have left your mother in ignorance." He shook his head. "I do not understand that. She should not be left to live in fear. I will not do that to you, I promise. If your father does not share with you what your settlement contains, I will." He looked toward the house as voices told him the Bennets were on their way to the church.

"I will tell you if he does, but I doubt he will."

Darcy moved his gaze to Elizabeth's face. He smiled, thinking he was a blessed man to have found a wife with such fair features paired with a generous and kind heart. "Shall we follow your family?"

"Yes, we shall." She turned her face forward. "I am looking forward to the peace and serenity of the service."

"I am, as well."

The pair ambled toward the church, trailing along behind the rest of the family. There was no time for further discussion, so they remained silent. Once at the building, they followed the Bennets in, taking seats in the family pew. Darcy found himself between Elizabeth, who sat on his left, and Mary, who was on his right. On the other side of his betrothed was Jane, who said not a word to anyone. And beyond Mary was Kitty, followed by Lydia, Mrs. Bennet, and Mr. Bennet.

Darcy had been surprised to note the absolute silence that overtook the two youngest girls from the moment they entered the building. He made a mental note to ask Elizabeth about it later, though from the severe look the patriarch gave his youngest daughter, he would not be surprised to discover they had learned through severe punishment to be respectful of God's house.

The service carried on as all do. The music was very good. *Surprisingly good,* Darcy thought, *given the small size of the congregation.* He was pleased to hear Elizabeth's lovely voice singing along beside him. The sermon was an original, which astonished Darcy, as most rectors he knew read sermons out of books written by others. Few took the time to create one based on their own personal study. Still, it was engaging and kept his attention. It did not hurt that the topic of the sermon was about judging others. *No wonder she enjoys church so much.*

At the end of the service, they all filed out of the pew and into the aisle to wend their way to the entrance to greet Mr. Pound and head home. Darcy had not paid much attention to those around him when they arrived, but he now noticed heads put together and fingers pointing in his and Elizabeth's direction. He ground his teeth and set his jaw, his spine stiffening. Looking down to check on Elizabeth, he noticed her doing the same, but with a small smile affixed to her face. He placed his free hand on hers to reassure her that she was not facing this alone. He was gratified to see her look up at him with appreciation in her eyes.

"Good morning, Mr. Darcy, Miss Elizabeth." Mr. Pound smiled at them and bowed. "I am happy to see you today."

Darcy noticed his betrothed relax at the rector's kind words.

"Thank you, sir. It was an excellent sermon."

Mr. Pound winked at Elizabeth. "I thought you might like it. In light of recent events and after hearing some of what I have in the last day or so, I thought it a timely lesson." He glanced around. "I hope the words sunk into some of the heads in my congregation."

"I do, as well."

Darcy grinned to himself at the wry smirk that twisted his betrothed's lips. He then thanked the rector and added his compliments about the sermon, and they moved past the man and out the door. When they reached the bottom of the steps, Elizabeth suddenly stiffened, drawing Darcy's attention. He looked to see her staring across the way, to a stand of trees near the road and a red-coated officer with his arms crossed. Immediately dropping her arm, he started toward the soldier but stopped when the other man spun around and mounted a nearby horse, turning it and galloping away. He shook his head and returned to Elizabeth's side.

"Are you well?" His eyes looked deep into hers, trying to discern her true feelings.

"I am." She worried her lower lip. "Thank

you for chasing him off. It startled me that he was here." She glanced around. "Did he attend services? I did not see him. Or was he waiting for me to come out?"

Darcy shook his head, reaching out to take her hand. "I did not see him inside, but he could have arrived after we did and departed before." He waved his hand toward the building. "This is not a large number of people, but it is enough that one person could potentially remain unnoticed."

"True, and we were rather distracted by the attention of the neighbors." Elizabeth moved her gaze from him, he supposed to take in the other people loading into carriages and beginning their treks back to their homes.

"We were." On impulse, Darcy lifted one of her hands and kissed the fingers. "I am sorry he disrupted your peace."

Elizabeth turned back towards him and smiled, giving rise to an answering gesture in him.

"Get moving, Elizabeth." Mr. Bennet's harsh voice suddenly sounded in Darcy's ear. "This is neither the time nor the place for such behavior."

Darcy frowned as his mien went from happy to blank. He glared at Bennet, who returned his angry look. The two gentlemen stared for a long moment, and Darcy heard Elizabeth shift beside him, indicating her discomfort. Finally, Bennet blinked and looked away. Darcy felt his chest puff up. He was determined not to allow this cold-hearted man to hurt Elizabeth any more. Silently, he offered his arm to his betrothed, never removing his eyes from his future father-in-law's retreating back.

"I am sorry." Elizabeth's whisper drew Darcy's attention a minute or two later. He looked down at her.

"It is not your fault." Darcy kept his reply quiet, just as she had. "You have no reason to apologize."

"I know, but ... it is because of me that his attention fell upon us in the first place." She shrugged.

"I will take full responsibility for that. I did not have to kiss your hand, though it was an impulse I do not regret." He paused and looked ahead to where the master of Longbourn strode toward the front door of his house. "The longer this engagement goes on the more eager I am to marry you and take you away from here." He frowned.

"It will be well. We only have three and ten days left to wait."

He felt her squeeze his arm and looked down, laying his free hand over hers and caressing the fingers. "Fewer if it becomes too much for you."

A brilliant smile spread over Elizabeth's countenance, and Darcy's heart raced.

"Indeed," she said. She looked forward. "Indeed."

Chapter 5

That evening, Darcy returned to Netherfield uncertain about how he felt. The afternoon had been exactly what he expected: chaotic and infuriating. He had begged Elizabeth, before he left Longbourn, to speak to her father about Mr. Denny. She promised him she would, but he was still uneasy. He entered his friend's home with his mind three miles away.

"Good afternoon, Mr. Darcy." The housekeeper curtseyed. "Mr. Bingley asked that you join him in the billiards room as soon as you are cleaned up and changed."

"Very good." Darcy glanced around, not hearing Caroline Bingley's strident tones. "Where is everyone else?"

"Mrs. Hurst and Miss Bingley are in their chambers taking a rest. I believe Mr. Hurst is in his, as well. Only Mr. Bingley is about at the moment."

"Excellent. I will join my friend as soon as I can manage it." Darcy nodded to the servant and then took the stairs two at a time. Washing off the dust of the road was the work of a moment, and soon he was changed into more casual attire: buff buckskin breeches and a green coat with a matching waistcoat. It was one of his favorite outfits. He loped down the steps and made his way to the billiards room at the back of the house.

"There you are!" Bingley's greeting was much more energetic than the one he had given in the morning.

"Here I am. You sound better." Darcy smirked at his friend as he strode across the room to choose a stick from the selection hanging on the wall.

"I feel better. Copious amounts of coffee and a nap during church helped." Bingley laughed.

"I take it you did not snore? Or has Caroline finished berating you for it already?"

Laughing again, Bingley replied, "I must not have, because she said nothing."

With a shake of his head, Darcy joined in the laughter.

"I spoke to Elizabeth about the events on the list. She says her family – her sisters and mother, anyway – plan to attend cards tomorrow at-" He pulled the list out of his pocket. "The Gouldings'. Then the dinner at Longbourn on Tuesday, your dinner here on Thursday, and at Purvis Lodge on Saturday." He handed the sheet of paper to his friend. "She has marked them on the list."

Bingley took the page and looked it over, then folded it up again and tucked it into his pocket. "Excellent."

"Also, while I was visiting Elizabeth, I wrote my cousin, Colonel Fitzwilliam, and asked him to attend me here. You had assured me that any of my family was always welcome, so I felt free to invite him."

"Absolutely! I will make sure Mrs. Nichols knows to prepare a room for him." Bingley tilted his head. "Is there a particular reason you have sent for him?"

Darcy nodded. "There is. You remember what I told you of that night at Lucas Lodge?"

Bingley's brow creased. "Someone chased Miss Elizabeth with a sword and you pulled her away from him."

"Yes, that is correct. What I have since discovered is that one of the officers of the regiment stationed nearby has apparently been following her. She has seen him twice in as many days, once yesterday on a walk to Oakham Mount and again today at the church. She feels his behavior has been unusual, and it has frightened her. I intend to have Colonel Fitzwilliam investigate."

"Good heavens." Bingley's mouth had dropped open upon hearing his friend's tale. "Poor Miss Elizabeth! I will keep my eyes and ears open; if I learn anything about this, I will let you know." He shook his head. "I cannot imagine intimidating a lady like that."

"Nor I, but he has." Darcy shrugged. "I wish I could do more to protect her, but until we actually marry, I cannot." He sighed.

Bingley was silent for a moment, then he reached for his stick. "Rack those up and let me see if I can beat you again."

~~~***~~~

Darcy spent a large part of the next day at Longbourn with Elizabeth. Though they were required to spend the first part of his visit in the drawing room, assisting her mother in putting together decorations for the wedding breakfast and listening to her complain about the circumstances of their engagement and how Elizabeth showed no care for the fragility of her nerves, they did manage to take a walk. Mary offered again to chaperone and agreed that Oakham Mount was a wonderful end point for their trek. Darcy made sure to thank her for her consideration.

"It is nothing, sir." Mary looked down and blushed. "I know we may seem cold, especially to outsiders, but Lizzy is my favorite of my sisters. I am ignored, but I have also learned to avoid notice. She is treated even worse than I am. She is abused and belittled at every turn. She does not deserve such treatment, and I am happy to assist her in her time of need."

Darcy looked at his betrothed and noted her thunderstruck expression. He gave his attention back to her sister. "I agree with you. Elizabeth deserves so much better than she has received. I have told her and will now assure you that I intend to put her needs first. It is my duty as a husband to see to her care and happiness and I plan to complete those tasks with my whole heart."

Mary smiled. "Like the scriptures say a

husband should. I like that. Thank you for your reassurance. I hope to one day find a husband that feels as you do."

Darcy returned her smile.

"Thank you, Sister." Elizabeth's voice wavered. "I never knew you felt that way about me."

"I could not give any indication of it, lest it draw attention to us both, but I have felt it." Mary reached out her hand to her elder sister.

Before Darcy knew it, the girls were embracing. He swallowed down tears. He had not experienced the same distance with his sister that Elizabeth and Mary did, but it was clear that both had been affected by it.

A minute or two later, the girls separated, wiping their eyes and smiling at each other. Darcy offered his arms to them, and Elizabeth tucked her hand under one, but Mary demurred.

"I do not wish to intrude. I will remain a distance behind, as I did before."

Darcy consented and soon, he and his betrothed were deep in conversation again.

"I spoke to my father last night, as you requested." Elizabeth sighed. "It did not go well."

Darcy's brows rose. "No?"

"No."

He looked down to see Elizabeth shake her head.

"He laughed at me and told me I was being overly dramatic. 'No officer is going to waste his time trying to frighten a penniless girl,' is what he said. He continued by reminding me of my fallen state and that I should expect attention from every man in the country after what I did. He then expelled me from his library and instructed me not to return." She clenched the fingers on his arm into a fist. Darcy placed his free hand on it and caressed it, hoping to calm her, though his own emotions raged through him.

"I am sorry. I do not understand his reactions."

Elizabeth heaved a huge sigh. "I do not, either. In the past, I have spoken of it to my aunt in London, and she thinks he is angry at how his life has turned out. He married in lust, not love, and never considered compatibility. Then, my mother never had the son that was required to break the entail. She grew sillier and he grew angrier. He left the raising of his children to his wife and the care for his estate to his steward and retired to his book room, losing more patience every year." Her voice grew angrier and angrier. "He takes his disappointments out on us, berating and belittling us at every turn. He has not bothered to save to add to our dowries. He cares nothing for us. And now, here I am, being hunted like prey." She stopped walking and took a few great, heaving breaths before she continued. "My courage rises with every attempt to intimidate me, but this is different. I feel that my life is in danger, and it frightens me to the bone."

Darcy squeezed her hand. "I am sorry. I admire you, though, for your bravery."

"Thank you." The corners of Elizabeth's lips tipped up briefly but then flattened again. "I hate to do this, but I may be forced to give over walking about the estate." She sighed. "I am undecided at present." She looked toward the edge of the path. "Perhaps it *is* only my imagination going wild. Maybe my father is correct."

Darcy turned to face her, causing her to mirror his actions. "I doubt that is true. You are an intelligent woman, and sensible. If you feel you are in danger, you are probably correct. I would like to see you suspend your walks, to be honest."

"I know you would. I may do it, but not yet. I did not see the man this morning, so perhaps he has gotten it out of his system." She shrugged, looking ahead and biting her lip. "I hope that is the case, anyway."

"I hope so, as well." Darcy pressed his lips together for a long moment, unhappy with what he perceived as her stubborn nature. In the end, though, she was her own woman and not technically under his protection. He turned them to resume their walk. "I received an express this morning. My cousin should arrive at Netherfield sometime this afternoon or early evening. He was required to attend to some meetings this morning and needed to get his assignments transferred for a few days to another officer, but his general gave him permission to come out here and help us."

"Oh, good!" Elizabeth sighed. "Perhaps with his military connections, he can uncover the reasons Mr. Denny is following me as he is." She looked up at her betrothed. "I simply do not understand what they could be. Is this related to what I overheard in the garden at Lucas Lodge?"

"It very likely is," Darcy replied softly. "I would imagine this Mr. Denny is involved in things he does not wish to be broadly known, and he fears you actually heard what was said and will expose him and his comrades."

Elizabeth shuddered. "Would I not have already done it, if I were so inclined? I did not even clearly hear them! It was more like I heard voices; I could not decipher the actual words." She huffed.

Darcy used his free hand to caress hers where it lay on his arm. "I understand your frustration and share it. Logically, you are correct. However, if he is involved in a criminal enterprise as we suspect, he is probably not thinking logically. My cousin is skilled in ferreting out information. If anyone can discover what is going on behind the scenes, it is he."

"I am glad to hear it." Elizabeth sighed again. "Please," she begged, "let us find something more pleasant to speak of. I should like to just forget for a while the danger I am in."

After wandering the gardens a bit longer, the couple and their chaperone returned to the house. Mrs. Bennet was preparing the teapot, and a platter piled high with small sandwiches and cakes was at her elbow.

"It is about time you returned. I thought I was going to have to send someone after you. Come get a cup of tea and then sit down over there where you were before. We have dinner with the Gouldings this evening but it is always better to have a mid-afternoon snack than to grow faint in public while waiting for the meal to begin."

"That reminds me of something." Darcy accepted a cup of tea and handed it to his betrothed before turning back to his future mother-in-law. "I would like to escort Miss Elizabeth to the dinner tonight, and Miss Mary, if she would consent to chaperone."

Mrs. Bennet handed him a second cup. "I see no reason to deny your request. Two fewer daughters in the carriage will give the rest of us room to spread our skirts out to keep them from being crushed." She waved him off.

Darcy accepted the cup, keeping himself from rolling his eyes, which he dearly wished to do, and turned to Mary. "What do you say, Miss Mary? Will you ride with us this evening?"

Mary nodded. "I will. Thank you."

"Excellent." Darcy bowed his head to her before stepping to Elizabeth's side and lowering himself onto the settee beside her. "What about you, Miss Elizabeth? Will you allow me to escort you?"

Elizabeth laughed. "I will. Thank you for offering."

~~~***~~~

Darcy remained another half-hour with the ladies. Then, he returned to his friend's home to await his cousin and prepare for the evening. He had not been back long before his valet informed him that Colonel Fitzwilliam had arrived, along with a pair of what appeared to be junior officers, and that the men had been placed in the formal drawing room to await him.

"Very good. Please see to it that a tea tray and some sustenance are brought to us as soon as possible. I am certain they are hungry after half a day of travel and whatever kept them occupied this morning."

Smith nodded and turned, exiting the room.

Darcy followed his valet out the door of his chamber and hastened down the stairs. A footman opened the drawing room door for him as he approached. He entered and strode forward, stretching his hand out to shake his cousin's, a wide smile splitting his face. "Thank you for coming so quickly. It is good to see you!"

Colonel Fitzwilliam grinned at Darcy. "Thank you for extending the invitation! I was happy for the excuse to leave the general behind for a while."

Darcy laughed. "I should imagine he was glad to see the back of you, as well!" He grinned as he listened to his cousin's mirth. He looked past the colonel. "Introduce me to your friends, if you please."

"Certainly!" Fitzwilliam turned to the strangers. "These are Captain Jeremy Sides and Lieutenant Jacob Grubbs. They are two of my most skilled officers. They are intelligent and skillful, and I trust them with my life. Sides, Grubbs, this is my cousin, Mr. Fitzwilliam Darcy of London and Pemberley in Derbyshire."

The officers bowed to Darcy and murmured twin greetings.

Darcy inclined his head toward the men. "If my cousin trusts you, I will, as well. Welcome to Netherfield." He gestured toward the chairs closest to the fire. "Please be seated. I have ordered tea and a snack. I am going with Bingley and his family to a card party at a neighboring estate this evening, and I believe we will be dining there. You are welcome to join us, if you wish, or I can ask Mrs. Nichols to have trays sent up."

Fitzwilliam looked at his officers, who shrugged. "Personally, I would rather stay here and rest up. I think I can safely say my men agree with me?" He paused, and when they nodded with murmured agreements, he looked back at Darcy and began to speak again. "If you will but give me a quarter hour to discuss the situation here, we can eat in our quarters and spend this evening discussing our options and laying out a plan of attack."

"Absolutely. I will ask the housekeeper to show you to your rooms and give her instructions about your meals; then Fitzwilliam, you and I can speak while I prepare for the evening. Say, in thirty minutes? I will check with Smith, but I understand that water to bathe in was already being prepared."

"Sounds good to me. Hopefully, there is enough of that bathwater to go around." Fitzwilliam's words caused his cousin and officers to chuckle.

Soon, the four had all retired to their rooms. Darcy's bath was, indeed, ready for him, and his valet had been sent to inform the colonel that their plan for speaking together was a sound one.

Darcy quickly bathed and washed his hair upon Smith's return. He dried off and began to dress, donning everything but his cravat, waistcoat, and tailcoat. He had no more than seated himself in his shaving chair when Fitzwilliam's knock sounded on the door.

Smith opened the wooden panel, and the colonel entered the room with his usual swagger. He found a chair at the small table near the window and pulled it closer, turning it around and sitting in it so he faced its back. "So, what is happening? Your note seemed serious, but was also rather enigmatic."

Darcy quickly filled him in on the events of the previous weeks.

"Are you certain about tying yourself to this Miss Elizabeth? Father and Mother may accept her in the end, but you know Lady Catherine will cause problems." Colonel Fitzwilliam's manner of speaking told his cousin that his concern was real.

"I am." Darcy tried to look at Fitzwilliam out of the corner of his eye, but Smith's hands and the razor got in his way. "You know how much I dislike the fawning of the ladies in my circle, and after what happened with Georgiana, that distaste has turned into a stomach-churning loathing."

"So you decided to marry beneath yourself."

Smith had just finished shaving his master and was wiping his skin when Darcy sat up and addressed his cousin.

"She is the daughter of a gentleman. In that, we are equal. It is not as though I am marrying a scullery maid."

"True." Fitzwilliam paused and Darcy noticed him looking him up and down. Apparently, he chose not to pursue it further. "Well, then. This Miss Elizabeth was chased by a soldier with a saber at a party, and the next day, an officer intimidated her. You do not know his name?"

"I do not know the identity of the one with the saber. The officer who has been intimidating her is called Mr. Denny."

Fitzwilliam nodded. "Do you have paper and ink I might use?"

"Certainly." Darcy looked at his valet and nodded.

Smith immediately turned toward the bed

63

chamber, returning in moments with his employer's portable writing desk. He handed it to the colonel, then turned and picked up Darcy's cravat and draped it over his master's neck.

Chapter 6

Darcy and Fitzwilliam spent the next half-hour going over everything the former could remember of the recent events. The colonel had many questions for him, helping his cousin clarify matters. Finally, Fitzwilliam was satisfied. He stood.

"I think I have enough information now to begin. My men and I will go over this tonight and will be ready to start in the morning. I assume you will ride out early?"

"I will, before I break my fast."

The colonel grinned. "You are nothing if not predictable. I will join you."

Darcy rolled his eyes, which prompted his cousin to chuckle.

"Enjoy yourself this evening. I look forward to meeting your betrothed." Fitzwilliam clapped his cousin on the back and exited the room.

Shaking his head, Darcy headed out of his chamber to see if his host was ready to leave. As he reached the bottom of the stairs and turned toward the drawing room, he heard Bingley hail him.

"There you are, Darcy. Are you riding with us to the Gouldings'?"

Darcy entered the room, accepting the glass of port his friend extended to him. "No, I have ordered my carriage brought around. I am escorting Miss Elizabeth. Her sister, Miss Mary, has agreed to chaperone us. I took the liberty of asking for your equipage, as well."

"Excellent! Thank you." Bingley grinned. "How is Miss Elizabeth today?"

"She is well. The situation has been a difficult one for her, but she is no shy, retiring miss. She is facing the situation with great equanimity."

Bingley nodded. "I am sure it has been challenging, but I am happy to hear she is doing well. I was impressed with her kindness from the beginning, but her poise that night at Lucas Lodge in the face of scandal was impressive."

"She is a treasure. I am quite pleased with my choice." Darcy sipped from his glass. "Did Mrs. Nichols inform you of my cousin's arrival?"

"She did. Where is the colonel? I was going to invite him along with us."

"I already did. He has chosen to remain behind. He brought two of his junior officers with him to help him investigate. They plan to strategize while we are gone and present their ideas to me on the morrow."

"I hope they find the perpetrator soon. No one should treat a lady that way."

The gentlemen continued their conversation a while longer, moving toward the seating area in front of the fireplace to join Bingley's sisters and brother-in-law and include them in the discussion.

Finally, though, it was time to head out. Darcy bowed and made his farewells to his friend, then strode into the hall to gather his greatcoat, hat, and gloves. He skipped down the front steps and nodded to the groom who held the carriage door open for him before climbing aboard. Soon, the equipage was rolling down the drive and headed to Longbourn.

Elizabeth and Mary were ready and waiting when Darcy arrived at their home. In a matter of minutes, he had been welcomed into the house, had escorted them outside, and then handed them into the carriage. He settled in the rear-facing seat, tapped on the ceiling, and they were rolling down the drive. They talked quietly for the half-hour ride to the Gouldings' home.

"My cousin has arrived from London. He got to Netherfield just a couple hours ago."

Elizabeth's brows rose. "That was fast!"

Darcy chuckled. "It was not fast enough to suit me, actually, but his general must take precedence, I suppose."

Elizabeth smirked. "I suppose so, since his general is essentially his employer and you do not contribute to his support."

"Unless you count the bed in my home, my cigars, and my stock of wine." Darcy tried to maintain a straight face, but was unable to once his betrothed began to laugh.

"I concede to your greater knowledge of his vices. He is, indeed, supported in part by you and should therefore attend you with greater speed." Elizabeth's eyes twinkled.

"Will we meet him, or is he going to investigate behind the scenes?" Mary's brow was creased, and Darcy understood her concern for her sister.

"I would imagine he will visit Longbourn with me tomorrow. He has brought two of his men with him. If I know anything about how he operates his investigations, he will send the officers out to poke around a bit in the morning to see what they can discover. He will eventually become more involved himself, and we may not see much of him until the problem is solved. He wants to uncover who is involved, because we know it was more than one man talking at Lucas Lodge that night."

"We do. There may have been three, even."

Darcy nodded. "I am almost positive there were."

Conversation then turned toward more mundane matters, such as wedding details and Mrs. Bennet's behavior.

~~~***~~~

To Darcy's relief, he and Elizabeth were greeted by their hosts and most of the attendees as though nothing untoward had happened the previous week at Lucas Lodge. He recalled Bingley's words about that night and wondered at the usual behavior of the

Bennets in public, since few seemed surprised by the events.

The evening proceeded as most of this type did. There were several tables placed around the ballroom, each with a different card game laid out on it. At one end of the room was a sideboard with plates stacked on top. Partway through the night, servants brought in pots and platters of food, cramming the top of the piece of furniture with every conceivable size of dish. The sideboard was moved away from the wall enough that footmen could squeeze in behind it, and they performed the office of filling plates for the guests as they became hungry and wandered over.

Darcy stuck as close to Elizabeth as he could. He paired with her at the whist table for part of the night, and then for lottery tickets, which they played with Lydia and Kitty. He was then persuaded to join a table full of gentlemen for a game of Commerce, which of necessity left his betrothed unattended. This would have been of little concern except for the fact that several officers were in attendance. He did his best to split his attention between the game and his future wife.

It was not until the end of the evening, when he, Elizabeth, and Mary were in his carriage on the way back to Longbourn that he learned exactly what had happened while they were apart. He listened in silence as his betrothed told the story, his jaw clenched. When she stopped speaking, he remained silent for a few minutes, gathering his thoughts – and his temper – so that he could speak to her without frightening her. "I had not noticed his presence, and I examined each of the officers carefully over the course of the evening. I am sorry I did not see him and thus left you vulnerable." He fought the urge to lean forward and take her hands in his.

"It is well. He may have been concealing his presence while you remained close to my side."

Darcy grunted. "I am sure you are correct but I cannot like it."

Mary spoke next. "I saw him standing behind you and thought he might be staring at you, but I was more worried about the game than an officer. I am sorry."

"Do not be."

The rustle of cloth told Darcy that his betrothed had likely reached out to her sister. "I agree with Elizabeth, Miss Mary. You behaved as you should; you attended to your cards and the company around you. You have nothing to be sorry for."

"Thank you, sir." She paused again. "I must ask: is Mr. Denny the reason you wish for my sister to have an escort when she walks out?"

"Yes, he is. This is not the first time he has unnerved her."

Elizabeth sighed. "It is more like the second time. The third if we count the incident at Lucas Lodge that brought about our engagement."

"Oh, my. What has he done?"

Darcy and Elizabeth briefly explained matters to Mary, who expressed her heartfelt sorrow at such a thing. "The scriptures say to do unto others what we would have them do to us. Clearly this man is not following that guidance. He is likely going to suffer similarly at some point, if he has not already."

Darcy smiled to himself, but when he spoke, it was with his usual serious tone. "I do not wish for him to frighten your sister any more than he already has, but I also wish he would do something that would allow me to go to his colonel and have him disciplined. He should not be out in public, menacing innocent young ladies. I am going to inform my cousin of this event in the morning. It will give him more evidence and will, perhaps, help his investigation."

"All he has done is stare at me and make me uncomfortable, at least so far. I do not wish him to do more, quite frankly."

Darcy grinned in the darkness at Elizabeth's tart tone. "I am sorry, my dear. I did not mean to make you think I wished worse on you than what you have experienced so far."

"Hmph."

Darcy suppressed a chuckle at her disgruntled utterance. The carriage slowed, and he knew they must have arrived at Longbourn. He remained silent as it came to a stop and the door opened. He stepped out and then turned, handing down Mary first and then Elizabeth. He tucked her hand under his elbow and escorted her up the shallow steps to the door, her sister having already scurried into the house. When they arrived at the top, he lifted her hand and kissed the back.

"You will give some thought to ceasing your walks altogether?"

Elizabeth hesitated. "I will. I make no promises, but for him to do as he did in public, at an event, was ... he frightens me beyond what even my usual courage can bear. Knowing that someone, possibly Mr. Denny himself, tried to kill me has shaken me."

Darcy felt an urge – an irresistible pull – to comfort her. He pulled her close, wrapping his arms around her. She was stiff at first, probably surprised, he thought, but then relaxed and leaned against him. He held her for several moments, "I am sorry you are going through this," he whispered. "I will do my best to protect you, I promise." The sound of an approaching equipage made him loose his hold. He leaned down to her and kissed her cheek. "Go on inside. I will wait to leave until I see the door close."

He felt Elizabeth nod and step out of his arms.

"Good night, Mr. Darcy."

"Good night, Elizabeth."

True to his word, Darcy waited on the step until the door closed. Then, he turned and skipped down to the ground and up into his carriage. He looked back at the house as his equipage pulled away and thought about the feelings of rightness that had filled him when he held his betrothed. He was eager to experience them again.

~~~***~~~

The next morning, Netherfield was in a bit of a flutter when Darcy and Colonel Fitzwilliam returned from their morning ride. They stepped out of the way of a line of maids heading up the stairs with their arms full of bedding and Darcy wondered what was happening. Hearing Bingley's voice in the dining room, he thought to pop in there and ask his friend about it. He gestured to his cousin to follow him.

"Good morning, Darcy, Colonel! How was your ride?" Bingley's greeting was, as always, cheerful. He shook Fitzwilliam's hand and welcomed him most enthusiastically.

"It was exhilarating, as usual." Darcy cocked his head and examined his friend. "You are more cheerful than normal this morning, and there seems to be a greater amount of activity in the house. What is happening?" He nodded to his cousin, who headed for the sideboard and began to make himself up a plate of food.

"I had an enjoyable evening at the Gouldings', which accounts for my good cheer. Also, my sister's suitor is due to arrive this afternoon, which means he will keep her attention and she will not stick her nose into my business as closely as she is wont to do."

Darcy laughed, shaking his head. "So the esteemed Baron Edgewood is visiting Netherfield. Perhaps he will take this opportunity to come to the point and make his offer."

Bingley rolled his eyes. "One would hope. I would imagine that my sister will find a way to make it happen, if he drags his feet."

Darcy laughed along with his friend at the thought of Caroline setting up a compromise or some other method to make the baron propose, though deep inside, he thanked God above that he never had to deal with it. He shuddered and then changed the subject as he followed his cousin to examine the breakfast offerings.

"Will you and your family be attending the dinner at Longbourn tonight?"

Bingley shrugged. "I believe so. Caroline will want to show Edgewood off to the neighborhood."

"You are still disappointed in Jane Bennet." Darcy looked over his shoulder, watching his friend's reaction. When he noticed Fitzwilliam's confused expression, he clarified matters. "Miss Bennet is nothing like her sister. She is ..." He sighed. "Unpleasant."

"Ah." The colonel lifted his chin and took his plate to the table.

Bingley sighed and looked down at his dish. "I confess I am. She is so beautiful, so serene.

I am still amazed that she hides such a vicious personality behind so lovely an image."

"I am sorry." Darcy did not know what else to say.

Bingley lifted his shoulders again. "All is well. I will get over it. It is regretful, but there are other ladies. I should choose someone from town anyway, someone who inhabits a higher circle than Jane Bennet. Or I should if I wished to make my sisters happy."

Darcy was silent for a moment. "I suppose so. I would hope, however, that once Caroline marries, both of your sisters will have more to occupy their time than they do now. They will hopefully be so involved in running their own affairs that they cannot run yours."

Bingley chuckled. "I would hope so, as well. Thank you for pointing that out to me."

Darcy grinned as his cousin laughed.

Chapter 7

The next few days passed quickly. Colonel Fitzwilliam's introduction to the Bennet family was everything Darcy expected it to be.

"Mr. Darcy and Colonel Fitzwilliam." Mrs. Hill announced the pair to her mistress and the ladies of the house, and Darcy could swear he heard a note of glee in her voice. Her countenance did not display anything untoward, so he dismissed it as his imagination. However, the effusions of Mrs. Bennet and her youngest two daughters gave credence to the possibility that the housekeeper had, indeed, found amusement in the announcement.

"Why, Mr. Darcy, I did not know you had any friends in red coats." Longbourn's mistress turned her attention to Fitzwilliam. "Tell me, sir, have you just joined the militia?"

"Actually, madam, I am in the regulars. I am Mr. Darcy's cousin on his mother's side." The colonel maintained a stiff posture, and Darcy wondered if this is how he himself looked when faced with uncomfortable duties.

"The regulars! Oh, my!" Mrs. Bennet giggled, holding her hand over her mouth and turning towards her youngest two daughters. "Even better than the militia, do you not think, my dears?"

"Yes, Mama. So much better!" Lydia batted

her eyes at the colonel, and Darcy fought to keep his from rolling.

"Cousin, this is Mrs. Bennet." Darcy gestured to the other ladies. "These are her daughters, Miss Bennet, Miss Elizabeth Bennet, Miss Mary Bennet, Miss Catherine Bennet, and Miss Lydia Bennet."

Fitzwilliam bowed to each lady, who curtseyed in return. "I am pleased to make your acquaintance."

"Do sit down, Colonel. Here, I will move to the table and you may sit beside my Jane. Is she not the most beautiful creature you have ever beheld?"

Darcy cleared his throat. "Actually, I was hoping Miss Elizabeth would join me and my cousin for a walk in the gardens, if Miss Mary would agree to chaperone again."

Mrs. Bennet huffed. "I do not see why you should want to, not when your cousin would like to get to know Jane better. If you must, you should take her as your chaperone instead of Mary."

"Mama-" Elizabeth began to speak but Darcy touched her arm and she quieted.

"We are used to Miss Mary, and we know that Miss Bennet dislikes the activity."

Darcy could see the indecision in Mrs. Bennet's face. She turned to her eldest daughter.

"Would you like to accompany Lizzy on her walk? You could spend time with Colonel Fitzwilliam and show him all your best qualities." She winked.

A slight crease appeared between Jane's eyes for a moment before it smoothed out. "I prefer not to walk, Mama. I am certain that when he returns, the colonel will be happy to attend me." Her smile was all serene contentment. If Darcy had not known it was a façade, he might have been fooled. He was happy he had warned Fitzwilliam of her true nature. As Mrs. Bennet started to fuss at Jane, he cut her off by turning to Mary and inquiring as to her availability to chaperone.

"I will attend you, if you will wait for me to put away my things." Mary stood from the table where she had been sitting and gathered up her quill, ink, and book of extracts.

"We will await you in the entry hall, Mary." Elizabeth gave her sister a barely perceptible nod as she took Darcy's arm.

A few short minutes later, the four were entering the gardens.

"Thank you again, Miss Mary, for accompanying us. Will you allow me to introduce my cousin to your acquaintance?"

"You may."

"Miss Mary Bennet, please meet Colonel Richard Fitzwilliam. Colonel, this is Miss Mary Bennet. She is the sister who is most like my betrothed."

The colonel bowed. "I am happy to make your acquaintance, Miss Mary. I have heard much about you."

Mary blushed as she curtseyed. "All good, I hope."

"Definitely good."

Darcy noted the look his cousin gave Mary and wondered at it, but shrugged to himself and let it go. "What path shall we begin at? I should like to end up in the wilderness area, for my cousin and I would like to discuss a few things with you before we return to the house."

"Why do we not skip the rest of the gardens, then, and go directly to the back?" Elizabeth pointed to the path that led to the pretty little area beyond the manicured flower beds where nature had been left largely to itself.

"Yes, we should do that." Mary stepped in the direction of the most direct route to their destination.

The four of them wended their way past the roses and chrysanthemums, the ladies holding the arms of the gentlemen. When they arrived at their destination, Elizabeth led them to a pair of rough-hewn benches she had begged her father to have made when she was a girl. The conversation that ensued became tense at times, but appeared to be a relief to both she and her sister.

"You have not made yourselves known to Mr. Denny, then?" Elizabeth bit her lip.

Fitzwilliam shook his head. "No, we do not wish to alert him to our investigation. We need to be able to go to his commanding officer with eyewitness accounts; events we ourselves have seen.

"I see." Elizabeth looked away for a moment, continuing to gnaw at her mouth. She sighed. "Will any of you be near in case of trouble?"

Darcy squeezed her hand, which he had taken in his own as soon as they sat down and began speaking. "In public, one of us will be close to you at all times, except when the ladies separate from the gentlemen after meals. I would like to post one of my cousin's officers as your guard, but that would make maintaining secrecy impossible."

Elizabeth's gaze searched his own, a crease making a trail across her forehead. "True."

"I will be near, Lizzy. I cannot do much, but I think with two of us together, Mr. Denny will have fewer options and you will be safer."

"Thank you, Mary. I will depend upon you." Elizabeth smiled at her sister.

"It is the least I can do." Mary blushed but lifted her chin. "Someone in this family needs to show some familial love. I am happy to be the one to do it."

"That is the way, Miss Mary!" Fitzwilliam smiled at her, and Darcy noticed that his cousin seemed intrigued.

The four spent a few more minutes discussing the details of keeping Elizabeth safe at social events over the next few days. Then, they returned to the house to visit with the rest of the family. It was the task of a moment to obtain an extension of the invitation to tonight's dinner to Colonel Fitzwilliam, and soon the gentlemen were turning toward Bingley's home to bathe and change before returning.

The meal at Longbourn went about as Darcy expected: it was a trial. The one at Netherfield two days later was less so, but only because there was a bit more room at Bingley's estate than there was at the Bennet residence and he could whisk his betrothed away for a little conversation in the next room. Two days after that was another dinner, this time at Purvis Lodge, which was very little different than any of the others.

What was the same, however, was that the officers, Mr. Denny in particular, were in attendance at all of them. The man never did anything that Darcy and Fitzwilliam could confront him over or take to his commanding officer. However, Elizabeth relayed to them at every event that Denny stared at her and made her uneasy. He always moved to the other side of the room when Darcy sought him out, so he was not even able to warn him off. He ended the week frustrated, though his cousin assured him everything was under control. His dissatisfaction was partially relieved when his betrothed finally assured him that she would cease walking out, even with an escort. He hated that she was distressed so much that she willingly gave up an activity she found enjoyable and necessary for her health, but he was happy not to have to worry about something happening to her when she was alone.

The day after the dinner at Purvis Lodge, Darcy once again escorted his betrothed to church. The colonel and his officers had gone increasingly underground as they narrowed in on Denny and his cohorts.

Darcy spent most of the afternoon at Longbourn, but returned to Netherfield to dine, having promised Bingley he would assist him in reviewing the proposed settlement Baron Edgewood had presented to him. That gentleman had done as everyone in the home wished and proposed to Caroline before two days had passed. Though Bingley was just as aggravated as anyone else at his youngest sister's manipulative and domineering behavior, he wanted to honor his parents' wishes and make certain she would be well cared for in the future. Darcy appreciated this quality in his friend and so was happy to assist him.

The next day, Darcy arrived at Longbourn on horseback, his cousin at his side. The gentlemen dismounted, handing over the reins to the groom that appeared at their sides. They looked around, thinking the house was rather quiet. With a crease in his brow, Darcy strode up the steps and knocked on the door, Fitzwilliam at his heels.

The housekeeper welcomed him inside with a curtsey. As he handed her his coat, hat, and gloves, Darcy tilted his head at the continued silence.

Zoe Burton

"Is all well, Mrs. Hill?" He caught the woman's eye.

"The house is a great deal calmer today, sir. The mistress has taken to her chambers and Miss Kitty and Miss Lydia are attending to her. Miss Bennet is in her room, as well. Miss Mary and Miss Lizzy are waiting for you in the drawing room." The housekeeper hesitated a moment, but then gave him more information. "There was an ... incident ... yesterday in the gardens."

Darcy's brow furrowed deeper. "I see," he replied slowly. "Is everyone well?"

Mrs. Hill's lips compressed for a moment, but all she would say was, "So they say." Then, she hung his things up, as well as the colonel's, and led him to his betrothed.

Immediately upon entering the room, Darcy knew that whatever had happened had involved Elizabeth. He watched her stand, her features pale and drawn and her arm held closely to her side. He immediately hastened to stand in front of her. "What has happened?" He reached for her hand.

Darcy no more than touched her fingers than Elizabeth leaned toward him and dissolved into tears. He wrapped his arms around her and kissed her hair, letting her cry it out. He looked to Mary, a question in his eyes.

With a glance at her sister, the younger girl explained to him what had happened. "She became frustrated with Mama yesterday, an hour or so after you left. She fled into the gar-

84

dens. She was not gone long, but when she returned ..."

"When she returned, what?" Darcy tightened his hold on his betrothed. A sense of impending doom washed over him.

Mary looked at Elizabeth again before lowering her gaze and speaking in so soft a tone that Darcy had to lean his head down to catch it. "Her clothing was bloody, torn, and dirtied and her hair was a mess. Someone tried to kill her." She paused. "None of us heard her screaming; I cannot even tell you if she did. Kitty and Lydia were so loud that I could not hear myself think. I feel terrible that I did not hear her, and more so for not going out with her. I might have prevented it, had I gone, but she insisted she needed time alone and she promised to keep to the gardens." Mary looked up and Darcy could see tears in her eyes. He ignored them for the time being.

"What? Who? Was it Mr. Denny?" He clutched Elizabeth even closer for a moment before easing his hold and leaning back to try to see into her face. "Elizabeth?"

His betrothed shook her head, which was still tucked under his chin and against his chest. She continued to sob into his waistcoat. He pulled her close again and began to rub her back, kissing her hair and murmuring to her. "It is well, Elizabeth. You are well. Shhh."

Darcy noted that Mary had seated herself on the sofa once more and was wiping her eyes with a handkerchief. Darcy urged Elizabeth to sit, as well, still maintaining his hold on her. Fitzwilliam, who had hung back, watching events unfold, took a chair near the younger girl. "Miss Mary." Darcy spoke over his betrothed's shoulder. "Did Elizabeth mention who it was?"

Mary shook her head. "She did not. I am uncertain she knows who it was." She reached out and ran her hand up and down her sister's arm. "My mother's reaction was not good. I suspect that is what has caused most of Lizzy's tears."

Darcy kissed Elizabeth's hair, his hand in a constant, steady motion up and down her back. "Should I ask, or will my imagination tell the tale on its own?"

One side of Mary's lips twisted upwards. "I am certain you can imagine it correctly. Mama accused her of having an assignation and setting out to ruin us on purpose. She is convinced Elizabeth did something to influence Mr. Bingley away from Jane." She shook her head. "There was a terrible argument. Papa even stirred himself from his book room to participate." She shrugged. "Neither of them cared that she was injured or that she was clearly terrified. Mama's only concern was marrying off Jane and Lydia, and Papa's was getting peace restored to the household."

By the time Mary was done with her explanation, Elizabeth's tears had lessened to quiet sniffles. She did not make a move to separate herself from Darcy's hold. Instead, he felt her snuggle in deeper. He kissed her hair again before quietly asking her about the attack.

Chapter 8

"I do not know who it was. I have never seen him before. It was not Mr. Denny."

"Were you able to see what he looked like?"

Elizabeth sniffed. "I know he was tall. His hair was dark, like yours but styled differently. He-, he-, he had a knife."

Darcy glanced up to meet his cousin's eye. "He spoke to you?"

Elizabeth nodded. "Yes, briefly. I do not remember what he said. I am not sure I even heard him at the time. I was terrified and fighting him with all I had."

Darcy kissed her hair again. "How did you get away?"

"I do not know. I was clawing at his face with my fingers and kicking him. He suddenly howled and loosened his hold, so I started to run. I did not know I was injured until I got upstairs."

Darcy's brow creased again. He pushed his betrothed away and began to look her over. "Where are you injured?"

"In my side. It is not deep, just a surface cut. Mrs. Hill stitched it up last night." Elizabeth shuddered mightily. "I hope to never go through that again."

Darcy chuckled to himself but his response was a somber as ever. "I hope you never have to. Has the apothecary looked at it?"

Elizabeth shook her head. "No. Papa would not allow him to be called."

Darcy gritted his teeth as anger rose up in him again. "I will pay for it." He thought for a moment. "I may call my physician from town to come and examine you." When his betrothed began to protest, he shook his head and interrupted her. "It will not do for you to become feverish. I am certain Mrs. Hill is just as capable of treating you as anyone, but a second and even third opinion would not go amiss." Darcy lifted his lips in a small smile. "I find myself dreading the thought of our wedding not happening, especially if it were due to you being ill or dead when I could have prevented it. I look forward to marrying you and demonstrating to you how a lady *should* be treated." He brushed her cheek with the backs of his fingers as he spoke.

Elizabeth blushed. "Very well. I cannot argue with that."

"I will ring for Hill. We may as well call Mr. Jones now as wait." Mary stood and nearly ran across the room, pulling the cord vigorously.

Darcy smiled at his soon-to-be-sister's sudden burst of energy, but then looked back at Elizabeth. "Part of me would like to confront your father about this, but my more rational mind tells me it would be a wasted effort. His demeanor when we signed your settlement on Friday made it clear that he wishes to be done with you as soon as may be. He will not respond well to my anger, and I will not hide it."

"He will not." Elizabeth looked down, and Darcy heard a sniffle. He lifted her chin with his finger.

"I am sorry. I know this is hurtful. The man who is supposed to be protecting you is not." He gathered her into his arms again, speaking softly but fiercely. "I vow to you, Elizabeth, that once we are wed, he will never be allowed to treat you poorly. We never have to visit here if you do not wish to."

"Thank you, sir." Elizabeth's quiet whisper was interrupted by the arrival of the housekeeper and Mary's instructions to that woman.

When the younger girl had reseated herself, Darcy spoke again. "Miss Mary, would you like to live with us? We will spend the season in town every year, and the summers at Pemberley, so you will not be able to visit Longbourn as often as you might wish to, but I am certain I speak for Elizabeth when I say you would be welcome. I have a sister who is around Miss Lydia's age. She loves music, and she would benefit from having a friend with sense who shares her interests." He looked down at his betrothed. "I also think it would help my future wife greatly to have someone familiar to her at her side as she learns how to navigate being the mistress of our homes. Do you not agree, my dear?"

Elizabeth nodded, giving her sister a tremulous smile. "I do agree. Please say you will come live with us, Mary." She held a hand out to her sister.

Mary's eyes filled with tears. "I would love to. Thank you for inviting me."

Darcy insisted at that point that his betrothed go up to her bedchamber and prepare for Mr. Jones' visit. He and Fitzwilliam went outside to wait for the apothecary, intending to speak to the man before he saw Elizabeth.

Darcy looked around to assure himself of their privacy before stepping close to his cousin. "Well, what do you think?"

Fitzwilliam's countenance was as serious as Darcy had ever seen. "She said this attacker was not Mr. Denny. I believe her, for I do not think attempted murder fits that man's abilities or propensities, not based on the intelligence my men and I have been able to gather. My guess is, Denny is not the leader of the group of men you overheard that night. It has been what, a week since the event?"

Darcy nodded. "Yes, a week exactly."

"I believe Denny was following her to discover her habits and routines. He probably reported his findings to whomever it is that is in charge and that man made this morning's attempt. The knife indicates intent to kill. This tells me that whatever they fear she overheard was illegal."

Darcy drew in a sharp breath. "I was afraid of exactly that. Have you no leads on who this person might be?"

The colonel shook his head, a scowl on his face. "No. Grubbs and Sides have not reported any meetings to me between Denny and anyone unknown." He paused. "You are not going to like hearing this, but we will have to wait and watch and be prepared for this person's next move."

It was Darcy's turn to frown. "You are correct. I do not like it. Not at all. I object most strenuously to this course of action."

"Keep your voice down." Fitzwilliam looked around. "We do not know who in this house can be trusted." He glared at Darcy. "The best I can do is to bring more men here from London. I know three who are experts in covert surveillance. They have served on the Continent and were injured. They are considered unable to fight, but their skills are such that they have been recruited by the Home Office. They are to report to duty there in the new year, so they have the time available now. I am confident they will attend us here and assist us."

Darcy sighed. "You trust these men the way you do Grubbs and Sides?"

"I do." A single firm nod accompanied Fitzwilliam's words.

"Very well. Please call them here. I will pay them well if they keep Elizabeth safe."

"I will leave you, then, and write the expresses." Fitzwilliam gripped his cousin's shoulder. "She will be well. You will marry in

93

a few days and live happily ever after."

"I hope so." Darcy watched his cousin stride to the stables.

Nearly an hour later, he was still pacing in front of the house when the apothecary came out. "How is she?"

Mr. Jones set his bag on the floor of his curricle and turned toward Darcy. "She shows no signs of infection at this point. Mrs. Hill is an excellent healer; I would have been surprised if the wound had been inflamed. It is tender to the touch, but that is to be expected when the injury occurred less than four and twenty hours ago." He lifted his hat and ran his hand through his hair before settling the covering on his head once more. "It is clearly a knife wound, and a superficial one at that. It will likely cause Miss Elizabeth some minor pain for a few days, but that should be all. It should not be debilitating. I have left instructions for her to remain still as much as possible and to keep the area clean, dry, and bandaged. The stitches will need to be wiggled once each day, and can probably come out in six weeks."

Darcy nodded. He felt lighter knowing that Elizabeth had been examined. Hearing the apothecary's excellent prognosis was like a weight being lifted off his person, one he had not been aware he was carrying. "Thank you. We are due to marry on Saturday. Will that be a problem?"

Mr. Jones shook his head. "No, not unless a fever develops. She should be fine, though."

Darcy blew out a breath. "Good, good." He pulled out his pocketbook and handed the other man a handful of coins. "Thank you again. You have set my mind at ease."

Mr. Jones bowed. "I enjoyed seeing Miss Elizabeth again. Since she has grown up and become a lady, I am not called to her side nearly as often." He chuckled. "She was a stubborn child and a difficult patient then. I cannot see that changing much now that she is an adult. I wish you well with her." He winked and climbed up into the carriage. Picking up the reins, he spoke again. "Call me if a fever sets in. Otherwise, I assume your physician in town will take the stitches out." At Darcy's words of assent, he nodded. "I would have him examine her as soon as you reach London. Good day." With a second nod and a flick of the reins on the horse's back, Mr. Jones was in motion, heading out Longbourn's drive and toward the road.

Darcy watched the equipage as it grew smaller and further away. He turned back toward the house and looked up at the second story windows. He went up the steps and knocked on the door. When Mrs. Hill opened it, he asked her to relay to his betrothed that he expected her to rest the remainder of the day and that he would return on the morrow. Then, he walked down to the stables to retrieve his gelding and headed back to Bingley's.

Upon arriving at Netherfield, Darcy retired to the library to write notes to his physician in town, as well as Mrs. Bishop, his housekeeper at Darcy House. He was interrupted when Bingley popped his head in the door.

"There you are!" Darcy's friend bounced in and plopped down in the chair near his. "How is Miss Elizabeth?"

Darcy hesitated. He was uncertain how much to share about what had happened. It would not do for the man who tried to kill his betrothed to go after his friends, as well, because they knew too much.

"She is as well as can be expected." He looked up. "I assume you have seen my cousin today?"

"Yes, he returned a couple hours ago, wrote some letters, and then left again. He seemed rather disturbed." Bingley cocked his head. "Has something happened?"

Darcy hesitated again but could not dissemble. He sighed. He would tell his friend the truth and pray for the best. "Miss Elizabeth was attacked yesterday in the gardens at Longbourn. She was injured. She is well and will be well, but she was frightened by the experience."

Bingley's usual smile was replaced first with wide eyes, then with a creased brow. "Oh, no! You say she is well, though?"

Darcy nodded. "As well as can be expected,

yes. The apothecary says she will make a quick and complete recovery."

"You are worried about her."

"I am. I find that the more time I spend with her, the more eager I am to marry her. She is ..." Darcy trailed off as he tried to find words to express his feelings. "She is everything I have looked for."

"You love her." Bingley's lips twitched, as though he were holding back a grin.

Darcy was startled at first at his friend's words, but he no more than opened his mouth to dispute them than he realized they were true. "I do." His eyes widened. "I do love her. How did that happen?"

Bingley laughed. "I do not know, but I suspect it happened quickly. You have often in the last month gotten a calf-eyed look about you when she was near. Before the evening at Lucas Lodge, even."

Darcy blushed but could not dispute his friend's description. He *had* watched Elizabeth a great deal when he first met her, and if he were honest, he still preferred to gaze upon her over anyone else. He cleared his throat and opened his mouth to speak but then shut it again. He glared at Bingley when the other man only laughed harder.

"Seriously, Darcy. Did you think none of us noticed?" Bingley wiped the tears from his eyes as he began to bring his merriment under regulation.

Darcy pressed his lips into a thin line, but he really could not be angry. He sniffed, narrowing his eyes for a moment before finally shaking his head and speaking. "Be that as it may, it never crossed my mind that I was falling in love with her."

"I am only happy you have. You deserve a good wife who loves you. Miss Elizabeth has a loving heart, from everything I have been able to observe. You will do very well with her." Bingley smiled at his friend. He jumped up and strode to the sideboard, pulling out a pair of glasses and a bottle of port. "We should have a toast to your happiness."

Darcy laughed. "We should." He accepted the glass of red liquid from his friend and stood.

"To Darcy and Elizabeth. May they be forever happy." Bingley lifted his glass, touching it to his friend's.

"Hear, hear." With a grin, Darcy downed a swallow of port. Then, he and Bingley sat back down to spend an hour discussing the progress of his wedding plans.

Chapter 9

The following morning, Darcy, his cousin, and his friend rode into Meryton. The colonel was expecting the men he had summoned to arrive on the post coach and he wished to set them to work immediately upon their arrival.

Just before entering the edge of the village and to Darcy's immense surprise, he saw Elizabeth and her sisters walking toward town. He and his companions pulled up and dismounted to greet the ladies.

Bingley did not tarry; after bowing to each of the girls, he excused himself, re-mounted his mare, and nudged her into motion. He needed some new gloves and was intent on getting them sooner rather than later, and Darcy knew he did not wish to be in Jane Bennet's presence any longer than he needed to be.

A huff from the midst of the group of ladies pulled Darcy's attention toward Jane, who was watching his friend ride away with a scowl marring the usual lines of beauty in her face. He strove to keep his expression neutral, but inside, he was smirking at the lady being thwarted in such a manner. He ignored her and turned his attention to his betrothed.

"Should you not be resting, as Mr. Jones suggested?"

Elizabeth's lips lifted in a small smile.

"Mama insisted we all attend our Aunt Philips. I have been careful, I promise."

"I see." Darcy turned to Mary, who stood beside her sister, a crease between his brows. "Has she been careful, Miss Mary?"

Mary darted a glance at the other three girls, who were watching the proceedings with interest, and nodded. "She has." She cast her eyes down.

Darcy also looked over at Jane, Kitty, and Lydia before he spoke. "Good. Good." To Elizabeth, he said, "We were on our way to Meryton ourselves. Perhaps we may join you?"

Her reply was lost in the sound of her youngest sisters' sudden exclamations.

"Lizzy, you must not keep the colonel all to yourself!"

Darcy watched as Lydia sidled up to his cousin and attached herself to his arm, eyes batting. "Good morning, Miss Lydia," he said. He watched as the colonel did his best to escape the grasping clutches of the young lady, stepping back the moment she touched his arm. She was persistent, however, even to the point of keeping hold of him as she curtseyed.

"Good morning, Mr. Darcy. Good morning, Colonel." Lydia smiled coyly at Fitzwilliam, batting her eyes again and pressing herself against his side.

"Good morning, madam." Richard stepped further away, grasping her hand with his free one and lifting it off his arm as he did. He bowed, then moved to Darcy's other side.

Darcy managed to not roll his eyes at Lydia's pout. He instead ignored her and addressed his betrothed once more. "Elizabeth?"

"I should be happy for you to join us, Mr. Darcy." She smiled at him and when he extended his elbow to her, tucked her small hand into the crook.

Darcy's chest filled with warmth as he gazed down at her. He felt his cousin move behind him and looked back to see Fitzwilliam offer his arm to Mary, which caused Lydia to loudly proclaim her outrage. The four ignored the other girls, choosing instead to step forward. Lydia pushed past them, rejoining Kitty, who was watching with interest. Jane had already begun walking and was a couple feet ahead of the rest. As soon as Lydia reached her, Kitty slipped her arm through her sister's and they moved swiftly forward, whispering to each other.

The group had not travelled more than one hundred yards when a shot rang out and something whizzed past in front of Darcy. He heard his cousin shout and turned his body toward Elizabeth, pulling her into his embrace. His horse, which had been trailing along beside and slightly behind him, startled, whinnying and moving about in such a way that he was between Darcy and whoever was shooting. A second shot rang out and then there was silence. He looked up.

Fitzwilliam had done with Mary what Darcy had done with Elizabeth. Darcy could see that his head was now raised. He knew Richard's eyes would be darting back and forth trying to see who the shooter was.

"Darcy!"

"Yes, Fitzwilliam."

The colonel let go of Mary, pushing her in his cousin's direction. "Get the ladies to safety. I will join you as soon as I can."

"I will. Be careful." Darcy's words were lost to the wind, for Fitzwilliam had already mounted his horse and taken off in the direction the shots had come from. He offered his other arm to Mary, suddenly realizing that he still held Apollo's reins. Thinking quickly, he tucked the leather straps under the arm that Elizabeth was holding, squeezing them and her hand close to his side. Once Mary had taken his arm, he set off at a quick pace, noting that the ladies were nearly running to keep up but deeming it too important to get them to safety to proceed more slowly. As they dashed toward the Philips', he questioned his betrothed. "Are you well, Elizabeth?"

"I think so." Her words were a little breathy. "What just happened?"

Darcy glanced at her, his jaw clenched. "Someone shot at us." He heard the ladies gasp. "Fitzwilliam is attempting to chase the culprit down. Miss Mary, are you also well?"

"I am." She fell silent, apparently focusing

on keeping up with his hurried stride.

Darcy nodded but said nothing. Within minutes, he was ushering the pair into their aunt and uncle's home. "I will return to escort you back to Longbourn as soon as I can. Wait for me."

"We will." Elizabeth stretched her hand to him and he gladly took it. "Be careful."

Darcy bowed, lifting her fingers to his lips. "I will." With a lingering look at her fine eyes, he backed away, then forced himself to turn and dash to the inn, where the post coach was disgorging its riders.

Though he had never before laid eyes on the men his cousin had sent for, identifying them was easily enough done. One had a patch over his eye, one was missing part of his arm, and the third walked with a crutch on a peg leg. He approached and introduced himself, informing them of his relationship with the colonel.

"He and I were escorting my future wife and her sister into the village when we were shot at. Colonel Fitzwilliam is currently searching for the perpetrator." Darcy looked around, a frown pulling his lips down. "Come with me into the inn. I will buy you a meal and summarize the situation for you. Hopefully, my cousin will think to look in here for us." Darcy gestured toward the door of the inn and the soldiers nodded, making their way inside.

Darcy was pleased to note the men choosing a table that afforded a view of the entrance to the room, then seating themselves in such a way that they could see the door. The long rectangular table was set a couple feet away from the wall. Captain Sheldon Rowles, Captain Derrick Mountjoy, and Major Bryan Meyrick took seats on the long side, while Darcy chose the far end. When the serving maid approached, they gave her their orders ... three bowls of the rabbit stew that was on offer for the day and four pints of ale. Then, they settled in for an intense discussion, keeping their voices low, though the room was not crowded, it being the middle of the day.

The men's meals had just been served when Colonel Fitzwilliam stepped into the room. Darcy stood, making note of the grim set to his cousin's mouth. The colonel immediately saw him and strode to the table, where Rowles, Mountjoy, and Meyrick were also standing. Fitzwilliam returned the men's salutes and indicated everyone should sit down again. The maid appeared at his side and he asked for a pint, smiling and winking at her.

Darcy rolled his eyes and shook his head but ignored the flirting. "Judging by the look on your face when you entered, you were unsuccessful in your quest."

"I was." The colonel shook his head. "It is as though he disappeared into thin air."

"He is familiar with the area, then." Rowles looked intently at Fitzwilliam, his spoon suspended above his bowl.

The colonel nodded briefly. "He could be. He is at least more familiar with it than I am."

Darcy's lips pulled down at the corners. "Did you see him at all?"

"No. Not even the back of his coat. There were prints from several horses, so I was not able to track him, either." The colonel glanced around. "He could be hiding in this inn somewhere, or in any of the buildings in town. Someone's basement or attic, an outbuilding, or even a rented room."

"Hm." Darcy was quiet for a long moment before suddenly pushing his tankard away. "There is nothing that can be done, then. I need to get Elizabeth home."

Fitzwilliam leaned toward his cousin and placed his hand on the other man's shoulder. "We will find him." He glanced around. "This is not the place to discuss it, but know that I will not rest until this person is dealt with."

"We will not, either." Rowles gestured to his companions, his mien somber, a deadly look in his eyes.

Darcy replied with nothing more than a tilt of his head. The men rose as one, Darcy heading back to the Philips' house while the others made their way to an open field at the edge of town, where they could receive instructions and strategize without being overheard.

Moments later, Darcy was knocking on the door to the Philips' apartment. When the servant answered, he gave his name, nodding his thanks when the maid granted him entrance, and followed her to the doorway of a smallish but welcoming sitting room. He bowed to the gathered ladies.

"Welcome, Mr. Darcy."

Darcy bowed again. "Thank you. This is a lovely sitting room."

Mrs. Philips blushed. "Thank you, sir." She glanced around. "I am certain it is nothing to your home, but it pleases us greatly." She paused for a moment before gesturing toward the furniture. "Please be seated."

"Actually, I am here to escort Miss Elizabeth and her sisters home."

"Oh, but we are not ready to go yet!" Lydia drew all eyes to herself. "We were just finishing our tea and Aunt was about to show us some lace she ordered from Uncle Gardiner's warehouse." She turned to Mrs. Philips. "Were you not?"

"I was, indeed."

Darcy pressed his lips together, glancing at Elizabeth as he did so. He could see from her expression that she was every bit as vexed as he was. When she looked his way, he saw her shrug just a little.

"Would it hurt to leave them here? They know the way home; we walk to town nearly every day."

Darcy thought a moment. The other girls had not been part of the group who was targeted by the shooter. Elizabeth was clearly the object, and whoever committed the act was probably not going to strike again today. He would regroup where ever he was hiding and plan a different approach. "No, I do not suppose it would."

Elizabeth nodded once and then turned back to her sisters and aunt. "I do wish to go home, so I will accept Mr. Darcy's offer." She rose. "Mary, are you willing to chaperone us once more?"

Mary stood. "I will." She turned to Mrs. Philips. "Thank you, Aunt. It was delicious." She stepped to the older woman's side and kissed her cheek. "I will see you tomorrow."

"Until tomorrow, my dear." Mrs. Philips sat down again and turned to the other girls. "Now, about that lace ..."

Darcy bowed before following his betrothed and her sister out of the room. A few short minutes later, the three of them were walking back to Longbourn, Darcy's horse again trailing behind at the end of his reins.

Chapter 10

The next day, Darcy's cousin was gone from Netherfield with the dawn and before Darcy could speak to him. The colonel had, however, left him a note.

> Darcy,
>
> I have set two of the men who arrived yesterday to guard Longbourn. They are hidden from view, so none in the house will know of their presence. The third is resting; he took the overnight shift last night and will again today.
>
> Grubbs, Sides, and I are continuing our investigation. We intend to observe the militia encampment for a couple days. I am convinced that Denny meets with someone regularly.
>
> Keep your guard up today, my friend. Until we know who this mysterious attacker is and can take him out, Miss Elizabeth is in danger. Potentially, you are, as well.
>
> Your cousin,
>
> RF

With a sigh, Darcy folded the missive up and tucked it into the pocket of his coat. Fitzwilliam was correct, and Darcy hated when he had to admit to it. He trusted his cousin, though, and was grateful for the man's willingness to lend his expertise to the current situation.

"Do you require anything else, sir?" Smith waited with eyes cast to the floor.

"No, not at the moment. I plan to remain at Longbourn the entire day. It will probably be late when I return, as Mrs. Bennet will likely invite me to dine with the family." Darcy rolled his eyes at the thought of his future mother-in-law, who he could barely tolerate.

"Very good, sir. Will you wish to bathe when you return?"

"No, just a ewer of warm water will be enough, I think. It will be nearly bedtime before I get back."

"Yes, sir. I will have one waiting for you." Smith bowed.

Darcy waved his valet away, then strode out the door and down the staircase to break his fast. He greeted Bingley as he entered.

"Good morning." He bowed, then made his way to the sideboard.

"Good morning! How did you sleep?" Bingley sat with fork suspended.

"Very well, thank you. Are you the only one up?" Darcy busied himself with filling a plate, then turned and made his way to the table. He seated himself, nodding to the footman who offered to fill his coffee cup.

"I am. Apparently, the baron's habits are much like those of my sister in that he believes morning hours are to be avoided." Bingley turned his attention back to his plate.

Darcy chuckled at his host's dry tone. He picked up his fork and prepared to dig into his eggs and toast. "How go the wedding plans? Caroline has not suggested a double wedding with me and Elizabeth has she?"

Bingley snorted, then coughed. He took a quick sip of his tea and coughed again.

Darcy reached over and slapped his friend's back a few times. "I apologize, old man. I did not intend to make you choke."

Bingley, finally having gotten his bite of breakfast to go down the correct pipe, looked at his guest from the corner of his eye before shaking his head. "No, fortunately. She has no desire to wed from Hertfordshire. She wants a grand London affair, and Edgewood agrees with her. Thankfully, your ceremony is mere days away. I will wait until next week to depart for town so that I can host you until then."

Darcy nodded, swallowing his mouthful and sipping his coffee. "Excellent." He looked back at his plate, picking up another forkful of eggs. "I plan for us to spend our wedding night at Darcy House. We will then spend a week travelling. I had thought to return to Pemberley at that point, but perhaps we should go back to London until after your sister's wedding."

"I know she plans to invite you. Whether you attend or not is up to you. I know she is not your favorite person."

"No, but she is your sister, and you are like a brother to me. I will double check with Elizabeth, but I do not see an impediment to attending. We can depart for Derbyshire immediately after, or the following morning, even."

"Good. I will plan on you being there, then." Bingley grinned, pushing back his plate and leaning back in his chair, his teacup in hand. "How goes it at Longbourn?"

Darcy shrugged. "As well as can be expected. After you left us yesterday, someone shot at us."

"What?" Bingley sat up straight, nearly tipping his cup over. Quickly, he set the delicate piece of china down.

Darcy nodded. By now, he had completed his meal and pushed his own plate back. He picked his cup up. "Someone, we do not know who, tried to shoot one of us yesterday. We suspect that Elizabeth was the target. Her sisters, except for Miss Mary, were well ahead of us. I am uncertain if they even heard anything. My cousin chased the shooter, but lost him."

"My word!" Bingley blinked a few times. "Was anyone hit?"

"No." Darcy shook his head. "Either the person was a terrible shot or we moved too quickly for him to aim accurately."

"Good heavens." Bingley shook his head. He

lifted his cup once more and leaned back into his chair. "How frightened they must have been! And you, as well."

"It was over almost before it began, but yes, it was very frightening. However, Elizabeth and Miss Mary handled it well. Neither of them dissolved into hysterics. You would not know they had been in danger except for the speed at which we finished our trip to Meryton." Darcy finished his coffee, setting the cup on the table. "When I left them at Longbourn later in the afternoon, I promised to spend today with them."

"Do you have another engagement this evening?" Bingley replaced his cup on the table.

"No, thankfully." Darcy ran his hands over his face and sighed. "It would seem that Mrs. Bennet and the rest of the four and twenty families in the area are content with the dinners and parties of last week, and we are not engaged for any further celebrations of our upcoming marriage. I am exceedingly pleased."

Bingley laughed. "No doubt. You have never been fond of socializing with strangers."

"Nor with those known to me, with the exception of my family and closest friends." Darcy shook his head. "It has been a struggle in the last week, let me tell you."

Bingley laughed again. "I imagine so." He pushed his chair back and slapped his hands down onto his thighs. "Well, my friend, what say you to a ride? I can accompany you to

Longbourn, if you wish to go there directly, or we can ride through the back fields here at Netherfield."

"I would enjoy your company on the way to Longbourn." Darcy stood, his friend rising with him. "I had hoped to speak with my cousin, but he is out already. If he happens to return before dinner, please tell him I wish to speak to him before I retire tonight."

"I will do that." Bingley followed Darcy out the door.

~~~***~~~

When he was let into Longbourn's parlor, Darcy could immediately sense tension in the room. While this did not seem unusual for this household, the degree of strain seemed much higher than normal. Darcy found himself reflecting the feelings in his own posture.

"Welcome, Mr. Darcy." Mrs. Bennet's words held a note of asperity. "Why does your friend never visit?"

Darcy's brows rose. He cast about in his mind for a reasonable explanation, but before he could formulate one, the matron continued.

"He must be a busy man, I am certain. That can be the only explanation, unless Miss Lizzy has had something to do with it."

Darcy opened his mouth to speak, but was stopped again, this time by his betrothed's hand on his arm. He had made his way to her side while her mother was questioning him. He looked down at Elizabeth, noting her shaking head, and remained silent.

"Mama, I told you, I have barely spoken to Mr. Bingley. It is not my fault that he has not called upon Jane."

Jane could be heard giving a sniff, which drew Darcy's eyes toward her. "Oh, I am certain you have done or said something. After all, you were behaving the strumpet at Lucas Lodge. He undoubtedly has decided that he does not wish to associate with our family after that."

Elizabeth huffed and planted her hands on her hips. "Oh, come now, Jane. I have told you a dozen times at least that I did not do anything wrong. What Aunt Philips thought she saw was not what she actually did see. If Mr. Bingley has suddenly decided he does not wish to call on you, there must be some other explanation. Perhaps he simply does not like your inclination toward negativity. He is, after all, a very amiable gentleman."

Darcy decided at this point that it might be best to interrupt. He could see his betrothed growing redder and redder, her brows drawn closely together. The hands on her hips had fallen to her side and were tightly fisted. He cleared his throat. "Why do we not take a walk in the gardens, Elizabeth? I am sure we could both use the fresh air."

Elizabeth clenched her jaw and Darcy thought she might object. He breathed a silent sigh of relief when her muscles relaxed and she turned to smile at him. The lift of her lips was small and taut, but he could see she made the effort.

"I think that is an excellent idea, sir." She turned toward the drawing room door.

Without being asked and with not even a glance at the rest of her family, Mary followed her elder sister out of the room. Darcy trailed behind.

After a long walk through Longbourn's gardens and down one of the paths his betrothed liked to walk in the mornings, the trio returned to the house. Mrs. Bennet had quieted, though she pointedly ignored Elizabeth and barely spoke to Darcy. She ordered tea, and soon, all of her girls, herself, and her future son-in-law were munching on small sandwiches and cakes.

"Oh! I almost forgot!" Lydia's exclamation was typically loud, drawing all eyes to herself. "Mr. Darcy, I heard a story about you yesterday. If even half of it is true, I daresay Lizzy deserves you."

Darcy stiffened. He felt his betrothed do the same. He wondered what story the girl had heard and from whom.

"It seems, Sister, that your betrothed was not his father's favorite, and that he stole a valuable living from the gentleman who was."

Darcy's eyes grew wide for a moment, then his brows drew together as his lips turned down. There could only be one person who would spread a story like that. "Who did you hear this from, Miss Lydia?" He turned to his betrothed. "I assure you that it is false."

Elizabeth's lips lifted in a small, fleeting smile. "Do not fear, Mr. Darcy. I am not worried."

"I heard it from a Mr. Wickham." Lydia turned to her next oldest sister. "That is what he said, is it not, Kitty?"

Kitty looked up from her sketchbook. "It is what he said." She cocked her head and looked Darcy up and down. "He made you sound like a terrible person. He was very persuasive, but you have never seemed to me to be like that. You did agree to marry my sister, when you could have easily left her to her ruin." She shrugged and went back to her sketching.

Darcy's attention was wholly on the youngest Bennet. "Mr. George Wickham?"

"Yes," Lydia replied. "From Derbyshire and London."

Darcy breathed in deeply. He felt his heart rate increase along with his temper. "Mr. George Wickham is not to be trusted, Miss Lydia. He is a rake and a liar and is skilled at making people believe what he wishes." Darcy shook his head. "And those are his good qualities. You would be wise to stay away from him." He stood and turned to Elizabeth, who had risen with him. "I must speak to your father and warn him. I doubt he will take me seriously, but I must try."

Elizabeth's mien spoke of her uncertainty,

117

but her words were supportive. "Indeed, you must. Come, we will go now and see if he will receive us."

Unfortunately, Mr. Bennet was not inclined to have his sanctuary invaded at that moment. Both Darcy and his betrothed sighed in frustration.

"I am sorry." Elizabeth looked as upset as Darcy felt.

"It is not your fault, my dear." He looked at the door with a frown, then back at his betrothed. "I need to write to my cousin. He was investigating early this morning, but may have returned to Netherfield by now."

Elizabeth nodded. "There is a writing desk in the music room. You can use the supplies that are there." She turned and began to hasten across the hall.

As Darcy entered the music room behind his betrothed, he noted Mary sitting at the pianoforte, sorting through the music. He smiled at her and inclined his head toward her, pleased to note her answering smile and quick curtsey.

"I see how fortuitous it was for me to decide to practice just now." She turned toward her sister. "Lizzy, I do not believe what this man, this Mr. Wickham, said about Mr. Darcy. I have had ample opportunity to examine his character in recent days, and everything I have seen refutes those horrible claims."

"I agree with you, Mary." Elizabeth looked

at Darcy, a soft expression in her eyes. "Mr. Darcy is the best of men, and this Mr. Wickham is, for some reason, trying to make him look bad."

"Thank you for your faith in me." Darcy closed the gap between him and his betrothed. Then, he grasped her hand and lifted it to his mouth, kissing the fingers. "It means the world to me."

Elizabeth blushed, but smiled at him before she looked down.

Though he wished he could hold her hand forever, Darcy let the small, delicate appendage go. He cleared his throat. "Paper?"

Elizabeth jumped, looking startled. "Oh, yes! I am sorry." She whirled around, and Darcy smirked at her flustered appearance. He followed her to the window, where a small writing desk had been placed on a table. "Everything you need is here. When you are finished writing, I will summon someone to deliver it. We usually call on Mrs. Hill's grandson to be our courier. He is only seven, but he is quite reliable and knows every inch of the area like the back of his hand."

"Very well. He will do." Darcy pulled out the chair nearest the portable writing desk and opened it, pulling out quills, ink, and paper. He examined the pens, choosing the best-looking one and trimming it, then placed a piece of paper before him, opened the ink, and dipped the quill in it. He chose his words carefully, but urged his cousin to attend him at Longbourn as soon as possible, or to await him in his chambers.

"Is the colonel also well-acquainted with this man?" Elizabeth had seated herself beside Darcy and he knew she could clearly see what he had written. He had made no effort to hide his words. He was not concerned at her knowledge of his private correspondence in this instance, especially since it involved her.

"He is." Darcy signed his note, sanded it, sealed it, and addressed the outside. He tapped it on the table as he looked his betrothed in the eye. "At the risk of alarming you, I must tell you that it is highly likely Wickham is involved in the attacks upon your person. He has been known to participate in criminal activity in the past. At the very least, he hopes to disgrace me in the eyes of your friends and neighbors. This has been his pattern these last four and a half years, though he has hurt my family, or tried to, in an even worse manner just this past summer."

Darcy watched Elizabeth's brows rise. "How?" she asked.

He stood. "Let us send this on its way and I will tell you."

Elizabeth nodded and rose, walking to the bell pull. When Mrs. Hill answered the call, his betrothed calmly asked for Jerry to attend her. Without a word, the housekeeper nodded, curtseyed, and exited the room. Within a few minutes, a small boy was knocking on the door.

"Please take this to Netherfield just as quick as you can." Elizabeth glanced over her shoulder to look at Darcy. "Should he give it only to the colonel?"

Darcy paused a moment but then nodded. "Yes, that would be best. If he is not there, you are to wait for him. His name is Colonel Fitzwilliam. Can you do this?"

Little Jerry's eyes lit up. "I can! Netherfield's cook is the best. She always has my favorite biscuits in a tin on her counter, and she is not afraid to share them!"

Darcy and Elizabeth laughed. Darcy dug into his pocket and pulled out a coin, handing it over to the lad. "There will be another just like this for you if you do exactly as I say."

Jerry reached reverently for the money, his eyes wide. "Oh, I will, I promise! You can count on me!"

"Excellent. Do you remember his name?" Darcy waited for the boy to reply.

"Colonel Fitzwilliam!" Jerry grinned.

"Very good!" Darcy praised the child while Elizabeth clapped. "Off you go now. Go straight to Netherfield and give this only to my cousin. Miss Lizzy and I will tell your grandmother where you are."

Without a word, the boy bowed and spun, heading toward the servant's entrance in the back of the house.

Darcy and Elizabeth moved from the doorway to the sofa while Mary continued to play softly in the background.

Chapter 11

The engaged couple settled on the couch, turned slightly so they faced each other.

"Tell me; how has this Mr. Wickham hurt your family?" Elizabeth's words were quiet. The crease formed between her brows told him of her concern.

Darcy sighed to himself. He wished he did not have to relive the event, but there was nothing for it. Elizabeth was marrying him in three days. She needed to know.

"I have a sister who is more than ten years my junior. Her name is Georgiana, and I share guardianship of her with Colonel Fitzwilliam. We sent her to school a couple years ago, but this past spring, decided to remove her. We hired a companion for her, a woman named Mrs. Younge. When summer came, Georgiana expressed a desire to visit Ramsgate. Mrs. Younge assured me that many of my sister's friends would also be visiting at the same time, so I consented. I arranged for a house and servants for her." Darcy paused and swallowed, looking at his hands where they rested on his thighs. He saw Elizabeth's small hand reach over and press his larger one. Without thinking, he turned his palm up, curling his fingers over hers, instantly feeling a sense of peace settle over him. With a deep sigh, he continued his tale.

"On the spur of the moment, I decided to visit. I arrived unannounced to find my sister and her companion more flustered than I expected. I excused Mrs. Younge for the day and while my sister and I were talking, she confessed to me that she had met Mr. Wickham one day while she and her companion were out. He had flattered her with his pretty words ..." Darcy could hear the bitterness in his tone but was unable to temper it. "And reminded her of times past, when she was a child. You see," he said as he looked into Elizabeth's eyes, "Wickham was the son of my father's steward. We grew up together and were playmates. My father was his godfather, and we were sometimes called upon to entertain Georgiana after my mother's passing. He knew exactly what to say to her to turn her head."

"He gained her trust in that manner?" Elizabeth squeezed his hand. "I am sorry for your pain."

"Thank you." Darcy's lips lifted briefly at the corners. "It gets worse. He convinced my sister that he was in love with her and that they should elope." He sighed. "You see, when my father passed away, he left his godson a sum of money and the living Miss Lydia mentioned. He was only to receive the living if he took orders. Not only was Wickham not suitable for the church, he declared he had no desire for it. Instead, he told me he wished to study the law and requested money in lieu of the living. I had to negotiate him down to a reasonable sum, but he finally accepted the cash and signed away all rights to the living. He came back last year, demanding the position."

Elizabeth's eyes were wide, her mouth falling open. "I hope you denied him!"

"Oh, I did. Most emphatically. I reminded him of the document he had signed. He became angry and began to abuse me most vehemently. I had him escorted from the property and warned him to never return."

"So, when he saw your sister at Ramsgate, he thought he had found a way to get his revenge."

Darcy shook his head. "It is worse than that. He wanted her dowry, and when he discovered that he had to have the approval of both of her guardians, and that neither I nor my cousin would be granting it, he again became angry, demeaning both my sister and myself. He left after bringing Georgiana to tears. She was heartbroken. In the course of investigating how she had even come to be in his sphere, it was revealed that Mrs. Younge had a connection to Wickham. She had applied for the position she was in at his bequest. Her references had been forged. I was appalled at how fully I had been deceived. We left the next morning for town and a new companion was hired, one that my cousin and I scrutinized quite closely. Then, Bingley leased Netherfield and invited me here."

"How is your sister now?" Elizabeth's soft question brought Darcy's eyes up once more

Zoe Burton

from where they had fallen.

"She is not as devastated as she was but her spirits are still low." Darcy rubbed his thumb over his betrothed's hand, as he had been doing for several minutes. "I have written to her about you. I hope you will want to be friends with her. She is a sweet girl. Nothing like your sisters." He glanced over his shoulder. "Miss Mary excluded."

Elizabeth smiled and followed his gaze to the pianoforte. "I should enjoy being friends with her, I think." She looked back at Darcy and bit her lip. "I have never really been friends with anyone before. I told you previously, as has Mary, that we were not encouraged to be on friendly terms with anyone. But I would dearly love to be your sister's friend, as well as a friend to my own sister."

"You are well on your way, Elizabeth. One of the reasons I chose you was that I could see the difference between you and the rest of your sisters. You were more open and honest in your dealings with those around you than your older sister or your two youngest. You will be a blessing to Georgiana, I know it. As will Miss Mary."

"Thank you for your faith in me."

Before anything else could be said, Mrs. Hill knocked on the door and stuck her head in. She opened the wood panel wide, stepping inside and announcing Darcy's cousin.

"Colonel Fitzwilliam."

126

Richard swept into the room, his keen gaze encompassing its occupants before settling on Darcy. "You called?"

"I did." Darcy gestured to a chair beside him. "Come sit. I have information for you."

Fitzwilliam's brows rose but he held his questions until he had seated himself. "What information do you have?"

"I suspect George Wickham is involved in whatever nefarious activities have caused Elizabeth to be a target."

The colonel's countenance immediately darkened. "Wickham. I should have known." He spat the words out, disgust clear.

"We could not have. My investigator lost track of him weeks ago. We had no way of knowing where he was."

Fitzwilliam glanced at Mary as she joined her sister and the gentlemen at the seating area. "We must discuss our next steps, but that can wait until we return to Netherfield, I think. I learned a thing or two myself today."

Darcy nodded. "Good. I look forward to hearing of it."

Just then, the bell sounded to call them to dinner.

"Will your mother mind another mouth to feed?" Darcy directed his question to Elizabeth, who shook her head.

"No, I doubt she will. She enjoys company and, as you have witnessed, has a special affinity for men in red coats."

"Just like our youngest sisters." Mary's interjection was met with chuckles.

"True." Elizabeth smiled at her sister as she rose. "Let us ask her now."

As predicted, Mrs. Bennet was not at all averse to having a gentleman in a red coat grace her dining table.

~~~***~~~

Later that night, once Darcy and Fitzwilliam had returned to Netherfield, they settled themselves into chairs in front of the fire in the former's bedchamber.

"So, what is it you learned today?" Darcy leaned back and settled his hands, joined together, on his midsection.

"I visited the colonel of the militia, Forster, today. I could get nothing out of him. Either he does not know anything or is covering up for his men." Fitzwilliam shook his head. "He did allow me to speak to Mr. Denny, who refused to give me any information. I tried every trick I thought I could get away with, but he would not budge. However ..." The colonel leaned forward. "I was halfway back to Netherfield when I was hailed by another soldier. He had overheard my questioning of the erstwhile Denny and, for reasons of his own, decided to give me the answers I sought." He paused and looked Darcy in the eye. "George Wickham is the leader of the group. He has not joined the militia but is a frequent guest at the camp and at certain soirees held in the area."

"Lovely." Darcy rolled his eyes and leaned his head back to briefly rest it on the chair. He sighed deeply, then turned his gaze back to his cousin. "If he is the leader of this group, there must be something in it for him. What do they do? Surely it is not a social club. Are all the members officers, or are some civilians?"

Fitzwilliam lifted his shoulders briefly. "According to the gentleman I spoke with, it is a theft ring. The officers are invited to the homes of the gentry and while there, they scrutinize the art on the wall, the quality of the silver, and the jewelry of the residents. They then return at a later date and steal the items that will bring in the most money. I got the idea they were all officers, except for our old 'friend'."

Darcy snorted at his cousin's description. "If Wickham is the ringleader, he must be the one to fence the items. Since he remains a civilian, he is at leisure to travel to town and back whenever he chooses."

"Indeed." The colonel paused. "This likely means, you know, that it was he who attacked Elizabeth a day or two ago."

Darcy felt his muscles stiffen and his countenance darken. His brows drew together as his jaw clenched. He breathed in deeply through his nose and then exhaled the same way. "Yes, I know. The minute I heard her sisters speaking of him, I suspected so, and as I listened to you just now, I knew." He hesitated. "And yet, we have no proof. Elizabeth has not met him and does not know what he looks like."

"We do not have proof. We will have to catch him in the act, as I had said before." The colonel held up a hand when Darcy began to protest. "There is no other way. We do not know where he is. We would have to draw him in in either circumstance."

Darcy slammed his fist on the arm of the chair. "I will not have Elizabeth put in danger. It is my duty to protect her, not expose her to risk."

Fitzwilliam leaned forward, his tone of voice urgent. "Be reasonable. She is all that will make him come out of his hole. She overheard *him* in that garden, I know she did. He does not know that she could not make his words out. All he knows is that she is a walking risk to his business and his safety. He will not do anything to you, or to me. You know this." He leaned back. "He must be stopped. Who better to do it?"

Darcy said nothing, instead pushing himself up and out of the chair and beginning to pace, dread filling him. He shook his head. "There must be another solution!"

The colonel stood. "I will be there, you will be there, and I have five of the best His Majesty's forces ever produced that will be there. We will protect Elizabeth or die trying."

While his cousin was speaking, Darcy had

stopped in front of the fire. He leaned an arm on the mantel and hung his head. "I cannot lose her," he whispered. He closed his eyes, picturing her impertinent smile and fine eyes. His heart clenched.

Fitzwilliam crossed the small space and put his hand on his cousin's shoulder. "You will not. We will keep her safe, I swear to you. If any harm comes to her, I promise I will allow you to do anything you wish to me in retaliation."

Darcy squeezed his eyes closed more tightly to keep a sudden rush of tears from falling. Though he fought the idea, he knew his cousin was correct. Wickham would only come out to harm Elizabeth, so she must be their bait. He hated it with every fiber of his being, but it must be so. He sniffed and rubbed his face on his sleeve before he stood straight and faced his oldest friend. Looking Fitzwilliam in the eye, he made his position crystal clear. "Very well. It will be as you have said. But let me assure you that if she is harmed, or heaven forbid dies, I will take it out of your hide." He turned toward the dressing room door. "I am going to bed. I will see you in the morning."

"I will not let you down."

The colonel's voice stopped Darcy as his hand reached for the door latch. Darcy looked over his shoulder. "I know you will not." He watched as his cousin nodded before leaving the room. Then, he sighed and pressed on the handle, letting himself into the dressing room. He allowed Smith to help him prepare for sleep, then climbed into bed, his mind full of Elizabeth and the possible results of using her to lure out of hiding the man who had become his greatest enemy.

After a long night of restless sleep and very little actual rest, Darcy descended the stairs bleary-eyed and out of sorts. He took his usual ride on Apollo, then entered the house via the door to the dining room, where breakfast was laid out. He filled a plate and began to eat. He had not been at it long when Colonel Fitzwilliam joined him.

Darcy waited until the servants had left the room to ask, "Shall we borrow Bingley's study this morning and develop a plan?"

Fitzwilliam nodded but said nothing else.

Chapter 12

Later that morning, Darcy made his usual visit to Longbourn. The weather had turned rainy while he was breaking his fast, so the usual mode of passing the day – taking long walks – was out of the question.

Darcy was welcomed warmly by his betrothed. Mary offered him a quick lift of her lips, and the rest of the ladies greeted him as they usually did, with brief curtseys, murmured words, and prompt ignoring. He paid them no mind and immediately seated himself at Elizabeth's side.

"How are you this morning, Mr. Darcy?" Elizabeth tilted her head, one brow raised and a smirk lifting her lips.

Darcy's heart skipped a beat. He loved it when she flirted with him that way. "I am very well, now." He took her hand and kissed the fingers.

Elizabeth blushed but her eyes twinkled. "Was the morning a trial to you?"

Darcy chuckled. "Every moment I am away from you is a trial, my dear." He winked, a grin spreading over his face as she laughed. "How are you? Is your injury better?"

Elizabeth grimaced for a moment but then smiled. "It is a little better, I think. Mrs. Hill seems to think it is healing well. It has already begun to itch. I strive to ignore that part." She laughed again.

Darcy nodded, squeezing the fingers he still held. "I have experienced that very thing. I will endeavor to keep your mind occupied elsewhere."

Elizabeth's soft smile made Darcy forget everyone else in the room. He longed to lean forward and press his lips to hers but Mary drew his attention.

"I am going to practice on the pianoforte." She looked toward her mother, who waved her away without breaking off her conversation with Jane.

Darcy caught Mary's eye as she left the room, noting her small nod to her left. He replied with a barely perceptible tip of his head.

Elizabeth's whispered words drew his attention. "Mary offered to chaperone again. I suggest we wait until she has begun playing before we join her. I assume you have things to discuss with me, after what we learned yesterday."

"I do," Darcy said in a tone just as soft as his betrothed's had been. "My cousin and I have come up with a plan to end the danger to your life."

Elizabeth said nothing, instead searching his face with her eyes. Then, she dipped her chin and sat back a bit. "The wedding decorations are done, I believe." She spoke now in a normal voice. Mrs. Bennet heard it and the next quarter-hour was filled with that lady's instructions and complaints. Finally, though, the matron was finished. Elizabeth immediately rose upon discerning this fact.

"I think Mr. Darcy and I will go to the music room and listen to Mary."

As she had done with her other daughter, Mrs. Bennet did not deign to break off her conversation to actually acknowledge Elizabeth, instead waving her away with a flick of her wrist. The couple said nothing else; they simply walked out the door and down the hall.

Once in the music room, they waved at Mary, whose head had come up when they entered. They seated themselves near the fire and began to chat.

"What is the plan you have concocted, Mr. Darcy? I assume you and your cousin have come up with something, some way, to draw out the man who assaulted me."

Darcy took a deep breath. "We have." He paused and looked into her eyes. "I would ask that you say nothing to your family members, for two reasons: one, the less they know, the less their chances of being hurt should something go wrong; and two, Wickham has already spoken to Miss Kitty and Miss Lydia. I do not perceive in either of them a particular ability to keep matters to themselves, so it is better if they do not know, for then they cannot share."

Elizabeth turned the corners of her lips down as she tilted her head first left and then right. "You make two very good points. I will say nothing."

"Good." Darcy grasped her hand. "We have determined that Wickham is the man who cut you. He is probably the one who shot at us, as well." He then explained to her what his cousin had discovered.

"So, he sees me as a threat to his freedom, I suppose." She shook her head. "I did not even hear what they said that night. I could not make it out. Can we not simply tell him this?"

Darcy was shaking his head before she even finished speaking. "I am afraid that will not work. He is convinced that you are a problem and he will not stop until you are eliminated. He was always rebellious as a child and at University, but he has become a much harder man in the last few years." He shuddered. "When I think of how close my sister came to being caught in his grasp, it chills my heart."

Elizabeth gripped his hand with both of hers. "She was spared a horrible life, and you spared her. You arrived just in time. Do not dare blame yourself for her hurt."

Darcy shook his head. "I try not to. I do." He closed his eyes. When he opened them again, he set his jaw and pulled his shoulders back. "At this moment, however, you are my concern. I must now save you from his clutches." He looked her in the eye. "I will protect you, Elizabeth. You mean too much to me at this point to do otherwise."

Elizabeth lifted her chin. "My courage rises with every attempt to intimidate me. What do you need me to do?"

Darcy laid out for her the basics of the

plan. Essentially, all she had to do was to go about her daily activities. He assured her that bodyguards were all around her, ready to step in at a moment's notice.

With a deep breath, Elizabeth promised to behave as though everything were normal. "Let us pray that he strikes quickly. I do not want our wedding put off if it can be helped."

~~~***~~~

Early the next morning, Elizabeth took up once again her habit of walking out. Darcy, Fitzwilliam, and four of the five guards were scattered around the path she had told her betrothed she would take. Lieutenant Grubbs, armed with a spyglass, had been assigned the night before to watch for Wickham from high in a tree just off the intersection where Longbourn's drive met the road. He had already warned them with a bird call that their prey was on the property.

Darcy trailed along behind his bride-to-be, hidden in the trees ten or twelve feet off to the side. He crept as silently as he was able, putting to use every bit of his skill as a hunter. As he tiptoed along, his eyes on Elizabeth as often as possible, he admired her strength. He knew she was terrified, but she never looked to the right or the left or behaved in any manner that would indicate fear. In his eyes, she was as amazing as she was beautiful.

Elizabeth suddenly turned a corner, out of

Darcy's sight. He tensed. He longed to rush toward her but knew he did not dare make noise and alert Wickham to his presence, if the man were even near. He forced himself to carefully choose the locations of his footfalls. A brief, quickly cut off scream made his heart stop. He immediately cast off all thoughts of remaining quiet and rushed forward.

Though it felt to Darcy as though it took forever to reach her, he knew that, in reality, it took only a minute or two to arrive at the bend in the path. He could see through the trees that his betrothed was struggling with someone. As he broke through them, he heard a curse from the man she fought with. Suddenly, Elizabeth was running back up the way she had come and Wickham – for Darcy could clearly see who it was now – was fumbling with her pelisse and a pistol. With a surge of speed, he threw himself at his enemy, tackling the other man to the ground. The pistol went off as they landed in the dirt, deafening him. He did not stop, though. Immediately upon landing, Darcy pinned Wickham to the ground and began striking him.

Darcy felt strangely detached. In his mind, he did not see the visage of his childhood playmate. Instead, he saw Elizabeth in the man's grasp, fighting for her life. He continued to pummel Wickham until he was suddenly hauled off of him.

"Enough, Darcy! We do not need you being

charged with murder." Colonel Fitzwilliam pushed him back, taking him further away from his enemy.

As his cousin's words penetrated his thoughts, Darcy began to relax, unclenching his fists and shaking his arms out. He looked beyond Fitzwilliam to see Mountjoy, Sides, and Rowles restraining Wickham, tying his arms behind his back and searching his pockets.

"Where is Elizabeth?" Darcy looked around, panic beginning to fill him along with a need to hold her.

Fitzwilliam looked up from his men to turn his attention to the road beyond them. "There she is. Meyrick and Grubbs have her."

Darcy's head snapped to the left. He closed his eyes and said a quick prayer of thanks before he directed his gaze toward his betrothed once more and started walking towards her. He could see Elizabeth let go of the guards' arms and break into a run. He stopped and opened his arms, closing them around her when she threw herself into them. He held her as close to himself as he could as she began to sob. Murmuring soft words of love and comfort to her, he kissed her hair. He did not know how long they stood there, entwined, but eventually, her tears lessened.

"I was so frightened," Elizabeth whispered.

Darcy kissed her hair again. "As was I. My heart stopped beating when you screamed. I was too far away, and feared I would not get to you in time." He tilted his head down in an effort to see her face, which was snuggled up against his chest. "How did you get away so quickly?"

Elizabeth sniffed. "He put his hand over my mouth, so I bit him as hard as I could and held on. I think I made him bleed." She buried her nose into his waistcoat. "I tried to kick him, but he must have remembered from the last time, because he kept me at arm's length."

"What did he say to you?" Darcy rubbed her back with one hand, though the other arm was like a steel band around her waist.

"He never spoke. It happened too fast, I think. He jumped out at me from the trees. I didn't really see him; he was only a flash in the corner of my eye." She shuddered. "He had a gun." Her last words were a whisper. "He cursed and then let go of my mouth. I took advantage and ran. I left my coat behind."

"I will buy you another." Darcy kissed her hair. What was the cost of a pelisse compared to the love of his life? "I came out of the woods just as you ran away. Wickham was fighting with the coat; it had wrapped around his arm somehow, but I saw the pistol. I tackled him."

Elizabeth lifted her head off his chest and searched his face. "You saved me."

Darcy could feel heat start to rise up his neck. "I could not let anything happen to you. I promised you I would not, and I meant to keep that promise." He lifted a hand to caress her cheek. "I love you, Elizabeth. I had to keep you safe, because if you had died, I would have done so right along with you."

A gentle smile began to lift Elizabeth's lips. She raised her hand to copy his gesture. He leaned his cheek into her palm.

"I love you, as well." She gazed into his eyes. "Will you not kiss me? Is that not what knights in shining armor do when they save the lives of maidens?"

Darcy's heart skipped a beat at her words. He could hardly believe them. "Say that again," he demanded.

"I love you, Fitzwilliam Darcy."

Joy filled his soul at her words. "Elizabeth," he murmured as he lowered his head. "My heart." He brushed her lips with his. When he heard her quiet moan, he caressed them again before settling his mouth on hers.

A throat clearing behind him jolted Darcy out of the pleasant haze he was in. He immediately lifted his mouth from Elizabeth's, taking a moment to allow his heart's rapid beating to slow. He looked at his betrothed's reddened lips and then into her twinkling eyes and felt the corners of his lips curve upwards. "Yes, Colonel?"

"We have the prisoner ready for transport to the local magistrate. We will need to have the apothecary tend to his hand. I want him alive for his trial."

Darcy nodded. He loosened his hold on Elizabeth, though he did not completely let go of her. He found he was very much comforted just by touching her. "Very well. As I understand it, Sir William Lucas is the magistrate at this time. Is that not correct, my love?"

Elizabeth nodded, glancing up at Darcy before addressing Fitzwilliam. "Yes, he is. Do you know how to get to Lucas Lodge from here?"

"I do not, but I would imagine one of my men does." The colonel smiled at her and bowed. "In case I do not see you on the morrow, welcome to the family, Miss Bennet. I can see that you and Darcy will do very well together and I wish you all the happiness in the world."

Elizabeth blushed but accepted his best wishes with a smile. "Thank you, sir." She looked up into the eyes of her betrothed. "We will indeed do very well together."

Chapter 13

Once Wickham had been led off, fighting his capture all the way, Darcy escorted Elizabeth back to Longbourn. The pair chatted quietly as they walked.

"What will your father say about all this?" Darcy was becoming a bit uneasy. They had said nothing to Bennet about their plan, and it did not sit well.

Elizabeth shrugged. "What could he say? You tried to talk to him about Mr. Wickham and he refused to see you. I doubt he cares. The event will not affect him in any manner."

Darcy sighed. "What you say is true, though the part of me that desires to do the right thing tells me I should have tried harder."

"There is no point in beating your head against a brick wall. It will only hurt you in the end." She looked to her left, into the woods. "I am only a worthless, useless daughter." She shrugged again and looked up at him. "Do we even need to tell him?"

Darcy was quiet as he considered her question. He sighed. "I do not know how to reply to that. I have no experience in dealing with such people. A true gentleman would not treat his children, even his girls, in such an apathetic, indolent, and cruel manner. If he were really a gentleman, he would have admitted me to his study, listened to my warnings, and taken them seriously. Part of me feels that he does not deserve to know for those reasons, but another part of me insists he be told, regardless of his previous actions." He shrugged. "Two wrongs do not make a right, you know."

Elizabeth sighed. "No, they do not." She paused. "I suppose, then, that we must tell him." She gestured toward her pelisse, which had been returned to her, ripped and bloodied and which she wore draped over her shoulders like a cape instead of in the proper, usual manner. "Certainly, once my mother sees me, she will raise such a fuss that he will find out whether we want him to or not."

Darcy snorted. "Very true." Seeing that they were approaching Longbourn's gardens, he stopped, Elizabeth following suit. "You are neither worthless nor useless, my love. You are intelligent and witty, charming and elegant, and a dozen more positive things. You would be an asset to any gentleman and I count myself blessed to be the one you are marrying. Frankly, the men around here must be fools not to recognize you for the treasure you are, but I am happy for their foolishness." He stroked her cheek with the backs of his fingers. "I never want to hear you describe yourself in such a way as you just did, because that is not you."

Elizabeth's eyes filled with tears as she listened, her gaze focused on his. "Thank you, my love." She lifted her face to his, and Darcy accepted her silent invitation, bestowing a tender kiss to her lips.

He forced himself to break off the kiss before it went too far. He brushed his lips over her cheek and then her forehead, then breathed in deeply. "Come, let us go face your family and discover the delights they will rain down upon us." He smirked when Elizabeth giggled.

"Very well, then. It is a good thing we marry tomorrow." Elizabeth peeked up at him.

Darcy turned his eyes from his betrothed to the path. "Yes, it is."

When they entered the house, all was quiet. Darcy suspected that the ladies were still abed. It was early, after all.

"Papa is likely in his book room." Elizabeth's voice was barely above a whisper.

Darcy nodded in response, following her to the now-familiar door and knocking.

"Come."

Darcy's brows rose. He looked at Elizabeth, whose countenance also displayed surprise, and noted her shrug. He followed her into the room.

"Good morning, Papa."

"Elizabeth." Bennet's lips turned down. "I cannot imagine what would bring you to invade my sanctuary so early in the day, and with Mr. Darcy, no less."

"Something has happened that we wished

to tell you about." Her hand crept backwards towards Darcy, and he grasped it tightly to give her strength.

Bennet rolled his eyes, as Darcy suspected he would.

Their interview with Longbourn's patriarch was brief. They informed him of the events of the morning, he made a few sarcastic remarks, Elizabeth countered with some of her own, and Darcy utilized the glare that he had perfected that made most people quail before him. In the end, they were summarily dismissed.

Upon exiting the book room, Darcy allowed his betrothed to lead him by the hand through the house to a back parlor he had never seen before. She locked the door behind them before pacing to the center of the room. She turned to him, hands on her hips.

"Tell me we never need return here after we wed."

"We need never return here, my love, after the wedding breakfast." Darcy cocked his head. "Do you still wish for Miss Mary to accompany us?"

"I do, if she is still willing. Do you mind that she will be with us on our wedding trip?"

Darcy bit his lip. "I confess I would like to have you alone, but she cannot stay at Darcy House by herself, so she will have to come with us. I do not mind it, truly."

Elizabeth looked at him with pursed lips. She cocked her head and raised her brows.

"Truly?"

"Truly." Darcy pulled her close, his hands on her waist. "I would rather she come with us than we be forced to return here to pick her up."

Elizabeth rested her hands on his chest, playing with the lapels on his coat. "Good." She paused. "I apologize for my father." She sighed and looked away. "And for my mother and most of my sisters."

"There is no need to do so. It is not your fault that they behave as they do." Darcy drew her closer, holding her tightly to him. He could not explain his need to do it; he just knew he felt comforted having her in his arms. He sighed before kissing her hair and laying his cheek on the top of her head. He heard Elizabeth sigh, as well, and closed his eyes with a smile.

"Thank you." She snuggled into his chest, her arms having slid around his waist.

A knock interrupted their interlude. They sighed and Elizabeth pulled away to walk to the door. She unlocked it and then opened it. Peeking around to see who was there, she stepped back to allow Mary to enter.

"Are you well?" Mary's eyes darted from her sister to her soon-to-be-brother. "You are fully dressed and not behaving as though you have done something wrong, so I must not have interrupted anything improper."

Darcy shook his head and chuckled, smiling when he noticed his betrothed doing the same.

"No, you did not. I am well." Elizabeth pushed the door closed. "We have spoken to Father this morning and it did not go well. I, for one, was angry, and Mr. Darcy and I stepped into this room to talk it over." She breathed in deeply, letting it out through her nose. "My anger has diminished." She turned to her betrothed. "Mr. Darcy?"

He nodded. "Mine has, as well." Addressing Mary, he continued. "Do you still wish to leave with us tomorrow? We will travel for a week or two before returning to London for the season. If so, we will need to ask your father's permission."

"I do, if you will have me. I know you will be on your wedding trip, but I will not get in your way, I promise. I have already received Papa's permission to go. I asked him a few days ago." Mary twisted her hands together as she spoke.

Elizabeth laid her hand on her sister's shoulder. "We would love to have you. We just wanted to be sure it was what you desired." She paused, looking at Darcy for a moment before addressing her sister once more. "We find that we have no desire to return to Longbourn after tomorrow. If you wish to visit, we will hire a companion to accompany you, or send a maid and footman or something. Is this acceptable to you?"

Mary let out a huge breath, then closed her eyes and nodded vigorously. "It is perfectly acceptable." She opened her eyes again. "I have no wish to return, either. I want to see what other households are like and to learn how to be a good sister, and to make friends. Maybe I can even learn what being a good wife involves so that I can one day marry."

Elizabeth smiled. "Good. Living with us will, I am sure, expose you to many other marriages and people and ways to live." She turned to her betrothed. "Will it not, my love?"

"It will. We will travel in higher circles than you have here and in more varying society. We will be pleased to offer you such an education."

A loud clattering could be heard on the stairs, and the voices of Kitty and Lydia wafted through the wood panel of the door.

"I suppose we must go face the rest of the family now," Elizabeth said with a roll of her eyes. "Am I presentable?"

Darcy looked her over with a critical eye. "Your hair is a bit mussed, but you look fine."

Elizabeth suddenly noticed his hands, which were swollen, bruised, and bloodied from his encounter with Wickham. "Your hands! We should have dealt with those first."

"What happened?" Mary's eyes had widened. "Were you fighting?"

"We will tell you later. He must at least wash his hands." Elizabeth turned to Darcy. "The water closet will have a ewer and pitcher of water."

The trio left the parlor, and the ladies waited outside of the necessary room while Darcy washed his hands. Though they did not look much better when he finished than they had before he started, they would have to do. He exited the room and escorted Elizabeth and Mary into the dining room, where breakfast was laid out on the sideboard. All three made up plates for themselves and moved to sit at the table.

Immediately upon looking at her sisters and future brother-in-law, Lydia noticed something amiss. "La, Mr. Darcy, what happened to you?"

Darcy exchanged glances with his betrothed. Before he could speak, Elizabeth summarized the events of the morning for the other three girls.

"Mr. Wickham attacked you?" Lydia seemed skeptical.

"He did." Elizabeth's jaw clenched. "He may appear all that is amiable, but he is an evil man underneath. Not a gentleman, I daresay."

Darcy quickly agreed with her. "He is not."

Lydia looked at Kitty, who had stopped eating to stare with wide eyes at Elizabeth and at Darcy's bruised fingers, and then shrugged. "You said he was taken to the magistrate. I suppose that means he will not be attending your wedding tomorrow, nor the breakfast."

Kitty sighed, apparently having overcome her shock. "We must do without his presence, I suppose," she said.

"We still have the officers." Lydia shrugged again. "They are ever so obliging." She giggled, and Kitty joined her in it.

Mrs. Bennet and Jane entered the room as the girls were speaking. Darcy braced himself.

"What are you speaking of?" The matron settled into her seat, casting a critical eye over her second daughter and frowning but saying nothing.

Darcy breathed a silent sigh of relief, relaxing his vigil, but only slightly.

Lydia began buttering her toast. "The officers, Mama. Since Mr. Darcy has beaten Mr. Wickham and had him arrested, we will not have his company anymore. Therefore, we must focus our attention on the officers again."

"Did he now?" Mrs. Bennet cast a disapproving look toward Darcy, but he, having anticipated such a thing, donned the same mask he had with Mr. Bennet, with the same results.

"Oh, well then." The matron paused. "At least there will be fewer of us to turn his head." She reached over and patted her youngest daughter's hand. "I was in love with an officer once, you know."

Darcy didn't bother to hide the roll of his eyes as Mrs. Bennet told the story of Captain Millar, with whom she had been in love before she met Mr. Bennet. He would be glad to leave this house and its residents behind tomorrow.

To Darcy's relief, neither Jane nor Kitty had anything else to add to the conversation, though he did catch venomous looks, aimed at Elizabeth, from the eldest Bennet daughter.

Chapter 14

That afternoon, Darcy returned to Netherfield to bathe and change. He had been invited to dine again and had eagerly accepted, keen to spend every moment he could with his betrothed. He was only partially dressed and sitting in the chair for Smith to shave him when someone knocked on the door.

"Colonel Fitzwilliam, sir." Smith bowed.

"Invite him in." Darcy waited mere seconds before his cousin entered the room. "Well?"

"Mr. Wickham has been seen by the local apothecary, had his hand treated, and taken to Hertford to be jailed until the assizes. I took him there myself, and spoke to the jailer. I stressed to him the importance of the prisoner and insisted he not be allowed visitors." Fitzwilliam pulled a chair up, turned it around, and sat on it, straddling the seat.

Darcy lifted a brow at his cousin's actions but said nothing about them. He tilted his head so his valet could better reach his cheek. "Meryton has no jail?"

"Not really. Sir William Lucas offered us the use of a room in his basement, but he is far too affable to be stern, and I did not wish to burden his household for that long, anyway."

Darcy could see the colonel's point of view, so he changed the subject. "Elizabeth and I are leaving immediately after the wedding breakfast tomorrow. We are bringing Miss Mary along. You are welcome to ride to town with us."

"I may just do that. Thank you." Fitzwilliam paused. "Miss Mary is going on your wedding trip with you?"

"She is." Darcy was still as Smith wiped the soap off his face. "Why?"

The colonel cleared his throat. "She could stay with my parents. Georgiana already is, and I know you would like for them to be friends."

Darcy splashed cologne on his face then looked at his cousin while wiping his hands. "Would your mother approve of you arranging houseguests for her?"

Fitzwilliam suddenly blushed from his collar to his hairline. "She will not mind. For one, she has accepted that I will not marry just anyone. I informed her only a month or so ago that I have a healthy fortune and do not need an heiress, and that I will wed whomever I wish to. She was unhappy about it, but she has bowed to my will."

"I see. This information, while intriguing, does not address the matter of houseguests."

"I wrote to her about Miss Mary." He paused, fidgeted in his chair, to Darcy's immense amusement, and looked at his hands, twisting them together. "I wish to court her." He looked up. "I cannot do that if she is travelling with you, or even if you are at Pemberley with her."

Darcy's brows had risen to nearly his forehead. "You desire to court her?" He heard the astonishment in his voice and wished he had tempered it, but he never expected his confirmed-bachelor cousin to want to court any woman, much less one with no fortune at all.

"I do." The colonel looked Darcy in the eye. "I felt an immediate connection to her when we were introduced. Though we have not spoken often, when we have, it has been significant. I believe my interest is reciprocated."

Darcy's brows rose again. "What, exactly, did you say to her?"

The colonel shrugged. "We spoke at first of you and Miss Elizabeth. I expressed a recently-experienced desire for marriage, she articulated the same, and we conversed about the goals we each have for the future and what we feel is important. Our outlooks are similar, as are our likes and dislikes." He paused. "I am not getting any younger, you know. It is time I set up my nursery, and it will make my mother happy. She will like Miss Mary very much."

Darcy nodded. "She is quiet and spends too much time with Fordyce, but she is proper and, deep down, has a caring heart. I suspects she longs for someone to love her."

Fitzwilliam agreed. "If she will allow me, I will do that, and I will treat her far better than her family does."

"See that you do." Darcy inserted as much sternness as he could into his tone. "You are a charmer and that allows you to get away with much, but Mary is going to be my sister and I will defend her as vigorously as I will Georgiana."

"As you should." The colonel leaned forward, staring earnestly into his cousin's eyes. "I swear I will not hurt her. I am serious about courting her. I wish to marry her. No lady has ever caught my attention the way she has."

"I trust you. I had to warn you, though, because it is my duty and I always do my duty." Darcy grinned.

Fitzwilliam rolled his eyes but changed the topic. "I will leave it to you to tell Miss Mary and Miss Elizabeth. It is not really my place."

Darcy nodded. "I will do it this evening." He stood and began pulling on his waistcoat. "Do you wish to come to Longbourn with me?"

The colonel stood. "Not tonight. I am meeting with two of my men. Four stayed behind in Hertford to question Wickham while one has been on guard duty, watching your betrothed, just in case. Two of the four are to report to me tonight. I doubt our old friend willingly gave up details, but Grubbs and Sides can be very persuasive, if you know what I mean."

"I do." Darcy stood still, allowing Smith to tie his cravat. "I doubt I see you before tomorrow, then, unless you learn something else."

The pair said their farewells, and Darcy

headed to Longbourn.

~~~***~~~

After the meal, Darcy and Elizabeth chose a settee on the far side of the room from her mother and sisters, settling in for a quiet chat.

"My cousin surprised me today with something." Darcy turned to face his betrothed.

"He did?" Elizabeth's brows rose. "How so?"

"It seems he is quite enamored of Miss Mary. He wrote to his mother about her and told me she can stay with Lady Matlock while we travel."

Elizabeth's eyes widened. "What does Lady Matlock have to say about it?"

Darcy shrugged. "Apparently, she does not have a problem with it. He wishes to court your sister and marry her at some point in the future."

"Really?" Elizabeth leaned toward him after glancing at Mary, who had chosen a wingback chair situated a few feet from them, closer to the fire. "Has he said anything to her about it?" She paused, tilting her head. "You know, I have caught her once or twice lately with what can only be described as a dreamy look. I wondered at the reason, but perhaps now I know." She grinned.

Darcy chuckled. "Perhaps. Will you tell her about his offer of a place at his mother's house?"

Elizabeth nodded. "I will, though if she

happens to join us later, you could tell her yourself."

In the end, Mary stayed near the fire all evening. Before he left, Darcy reminded his betrothed of her promise to relay the message to her sister. Then, with a glance around to make sure they were alone, he hugged her tightly, bestowing a brief but passionate kiss on her lips, before leaving the house.

~~~***~~~

Darcy's wedding day dawned clear and cold but with the promise of a warm up for the afternoon. He looked out his window at the trees, some of which had lost their leaves already. The majority, however, were clothed in glorious reds, golds, and browns. He smiled to himself. Deep down in his soul, he felt happiness such as he had never felt before, and he knew it was because this was the day he would marry his enchanting Elizabeth.

A knock on the door to his bedchamber brought him out of his reverie.

"Come," he called, inviting the visitor in.

Bingley poked his head around the edge of the wood panel before stepping inside. "Good morning," he said. "Nervous?"

Darcy laughed. "No. Excited." He grinned. "What brings you to my room so early?" He gestured toward the chairs in front of the fire.

Bingley took up his friend's silent invitation

and chose a chair to sit in. He looked up at Darcy as the gentleman seated himself in the one opposite. "Will it offend you if my family and I leave right after the wedding?"

Darcy tilted his head. "You wish to skip the breakfast?"

"I do." Bingley blushed and moved uncomfortably. Darcy had rarely seen his friend so discomposed. "I have every intention of supporting and honoring you and your marriage. I am proud to do so, and proud of you for what is proving to be an excellent choice."

"But you wish to avoid Miss Bennet."

"There are other reasons, as well, but yes, I do." Bingley shook his head. "I showed her a great deal of attention when I first came to Netherfield, but it has been a fortnight since she showed her true self and I stopped doing so. I mean, I do not think I attended to her enough to make an offer from me a settled thing, but every time I have seen her ... well, her and her mother ... at a dinner or card party or what have you, she attaches herself to me. It is clear that she has set her cap at me. You would think that two weeks of being ignored would make her understand I am not interested, but ..." He trailed off.

"It has not." Darcy's words were quiet. "I am sorry she has made you so uncomfortable."

"It is not your fault. If anyone is to blame, she is." Bingley shrugged. "Anyway, I am not at all certain she would not attempt to compromise

159

me right there in her own home and in front of her parents, and I am positive neither of them would object if she did. Plus, Caroline and Edgewood have been after me to return to town for days. They have done all the planning for the wedding that is possible from Netherfield and wish to do the rest from London."

"Unfortunately, you are likely correct about Miss Bennet. I completely understand your position and your sister's desire to go back to London. I am glad you will stand up with me. Feel free to leave after the ceremony. I will see you in town, though, after my wedding trip?"

Bingley laughed, a grin on his face. "Oh, certainly! I would be upset if we did not. I look forward to it."

Darcy smiled. "Excellent! I will send a note around as soon as I arrive in town." He stood.

Bingley jumped up. "I should go so you can prepare. I will wait for you in the entry hall unless I see you elsewhere in the house before it is time to go to the church."

Once his friend had gone, Darcy entered his dressing room, where his valet had a hot bath ready and waiting. He sank into it gratefully, appreciative of the effort and time taken by the staff to help him begin his special day in so delightful a manner. Once bathed, he dressed.

Smith seemed to take extra care with his master's grooming and clothing, tying the cravat in one of the more extravagant knots that were currently stylish and brushing the merest hint of lint off the dark blue coat. When he appeared to finally be convinced he had made Darcy as perfectly turned out as he could, he stepped back. With his eyes on the floor, he cleared his throat. "I wanted to wish you happy today, sir. Congratulations on your marriage. The staff hired from the area has nothing but good things to say about Miss Elizabeth, and I am convinced you will do well together."

Darcy was surprised. His long-time servant rarely, if ever, made any personal remarks to him. "Thank you. I am pleased to hear that my betrothed is thought so well of." He tipped his head. "And thank you for your congratulations. They are much appreciated." He held his hand out, giving Smith's a firm shake when the valet mimicked the gesture.

"I will finish packing and have the carriage loaded so it is ready when you are." Smith bowed, red-faced, and backed out of the room.

Darcy smirked as he watched his valet leave. He shook his head, then exited the room himself, descending the stairs to break his fast. As usual, the Hursts, Miss Bingley, and the baron were nowhere to be seen. Not even Bingley was there yet. Darcy did not mind. He made up a plate and took it to the table, seating himself and eating a leisurely breakfast. His thoughts were full of Elizabeth and the upcoming wedding, so full that he ignored the newspaper folded up beside his plate.

Eventually, Bingley did join him, as did the

rest of the party. Darcy and Bingley were the first to leave the house, in Darcy's carriage. Bingley's family would follow later in Edgewood's barouche.

Finally, the gentlemen arrived at the church, taking their places at the front. Within minutes, the Bennets followed. Elizabeth, Mary, and Mr. Bennet did not enter the sanctuary, but Darcy knew from discussions he had with his betrothed the last fortnight that they would slip into an anteroom off the narthex until the guests had all arrived and the music cued her to enter the sanctuary.

From the moment she appeared, Darcy was captivated by Elizabeth. She wore a new gown in a color that complemented her complexion, and it and the smile that covered her face from ear to ear made her glow. He was hardpressed to pay attention to the service, so fully did she capture his attention.

Chapter 15

Finally, the words had been spoken, the prayers had been said, the sermon sat through, and the register signed. She was his, and Darcy could not be happier as he escorted his new wife down the aisle and out the church door. The attendees stood outside, tossing seeds and rice and cheering. At the end of the line of neighbors stood Bingley, with Caroline, Louisa, Hurst, and Edgewood beside him.

"Congratulations, man!" Bingley slapped his friend on the shoulder. Then, he bowed to Elizabeth. "Congratulations to you, as well, Mrs. Darcy. My friend is an excellent man; a gentleman in the truest sense of the word. As I told him this morning, I think the two of you will do very well together."

Elizabeth smiled. "Thank you." She glanced up at Darcy. "I agree." Looking back at Bingley, she added, "Do make sure you get to Longbourn as early as possible." She looked over her shoulder. "Lest the food all be gone before you get there." She laughed.

"Actually, my love, Bingley asked me this morning if I minded if he and his party skipped the breakfast. I do not mind and I did not think you would, so I told him to go ahead."

Elizabeth's mouth made an O. "Oh, I apologize. I do not mind at all." She paused for a moment. "I am sorry if Jane's behavior has made you uncomfortable."

Bingley smiled. "You are quick, Mrs. Darcy. You will definitely do well with my friend." He laughed. "Thank you for your grace. It will not be farewell forever, though. Darcy has already promised to let me know when you get back to town. We will dine together, and perhaps, if you are still in London at the time, you can attend my sister's wedding."

"Of course!" Elizabeth smiled again. "Thank you for standing up with Mr. Darcy."

The parties separated then, with one group ascending into their carriage and Darcy and Elizabeth walking the short distance to Longbourn House.

Hours later, after chatting with the guests, avoiding the Bennets as much as possible, and eating as much as they could manage, Darcy and Elizabeth entered his travelling coach with Mary and Colonel Fitzwilliam, who were dropped off at Matlock House immediately upon their arrival in London.

~~~***~~~

The happy couple spent their wedding night at Darcy House. The staff, who had been alerted well ahead of time, greeted the new mistress respectfully, if not without a measure of caution. Darcy was aware that they probably had concerns about her, given the speed of their union and the fact that Elizabeth was completely unknown in his circle. He could not care less about their opinions, however, as long as they kept to their place and served him and his family well.

The first full morning of marriage was spent in the carriage on the way to Bath. There they spent a full week getting to know each other better and exploring the delights of the town.

When they finally arrived back in London, Mary and Georgiana joined them, their presence first announced by the arrival of their luggage. Darcy and Elizabeth were delighted to discover that the girls had bonded over music. Despite their age gap, with Mary being the elder by three years, they had become nearly inseparable.

Unsurprisingly, Colonel Fitzwilliam visited nearly every day. Though Darcy kept a room at the ready for him to stay in, and the colonel had often in the past availed himself of it, with Mary living there, he could not spend the night. He refused to do anything that might either offend her or damage her reputation.

"I am glad to hear it." Elizabeth settled herself more fully in Darcy's lap. They were in their sitting room, where they often liked to spend an hour or so in the afternoon. "It means he will honor her and she will have a better marriage than the one we witnessed at Longbourn. Lady Matlock likes her?"

"She does, but you will learn that for yourself tonight. She wrote to me, inviting us to Matlock House to dine, and I accepted."

Elizabeth's brows rose and he thought she might rebuke him for being overbearing, but all she did was smirk and thank him for telling her. "Her note indicated her delight with Mary's manners and modesty."

Elizabeth stopped playing with the hair that touched her husband's collar in the back. "Manners and modesty," she repeated. She tilted her head this way and that as she thought. "Yes, I can see her being described thusly. She does tend to be demure. My mother blamed that on Fordyce." She shrugged. "Perhaps it was so, but it is an excellent trait in a young woman." She resumed her play with Darcy's hair.

"I am sorry." Darcy rubbed a hand up and down her back. "I did not mean to bring up unpleasant memories."

"All is well." When he snorted, she looked him in the eye. "Truly, I am well. The longer I am away from Longbourn, the quieter those voices and memories become." She let go of his hair again, this time wrapping her arms around his neck and leaning her head close to his. "They are being replaced by the words and love of a good man, one who values me exactly as I am." She kissed him softly.

Darcy wrapped his arms around his wife, returning her kiss and then deepening it. When they parted, he retained his hold on her, sighing a deep sigh of happiness to have her in such a position. "I love you, Elizabeth. I wish I could wipe out the memories of your life in your parents' home, but all I can do is continue to make new ones with you."

"That is more than enough, my love." She snuggled deep into his embrace, where she stayed until it was time to dress for dinner.

~~~***~~~

That evening, Darcy proudly escorted his new wife and his sisters into his uncle's home.

"Darcy! Let me look at you!" Lord Matlock shook his nephew's hand and then held him by his shoulders. "You are practically glowing! Marriage suits you." He turned to Elizabeth. "Will you introduce me to the lady who has caused this happiness?"

"Certainly. This is my wife, Mrs. Elizabeth Darcy. My love, this is my uncle, Henry Fitzwilliam, the Earl of Matlock."

Elizabeth smiled and curtseyed. "I am pleased to make your acquaintance. Mr. Darcy has told me he is very fond of you and I can certainly see why."

The earl bowed, taking his new niece's hand and kissing the back. "And I can already see why he is so fond of you." He grinned and turned back to his nephew. "She is delightful."

"Of course she is." Darcy smiled down at his wife.

"What are you doing out here? Are you planning on allowing our guests to enter the drawing room, Father?" Colonel Fitzwilliam called as he stepped out into the hallway from a room further down. He strode forward, taking Mary's hand in his and tucking it into the crook of his elbow before his father had finished greeting her.

"Of course I am. I had to meet Mrs. Darcy first, though." Lord Matlock winked at Georgiana as he held his elbow out to her, grinning when she giggled.

The colonel snorted. "Took you long enough." He stepped toward the drawing room, immediately leaning his head down to whisper something to Mary.

Darcy chuckled and looked at his uncle. "I suppose we should follow." When Matlock waved him on, he and Elizabeth began strolling in his cousin's footsteps, the earl and Georgiana bringing up the rear.

As expected, Lady Matlock was every bit as delighted with Elizabeth as her husband was. They enjoyed a brief period of lively conversation before being called in to dine, and the enjoyment continued throughout the meal.

When the ladies left the gentlemen and returned to the drawing room, Fitzwilliam had news for Darcy. He had informed his father of all that had occurred in Hertfordshire, so there was no need for secrecy.

"As much as it pains me to say this, because I wanted him to go to trial and hang, Wickham is dead."

Darcy's eyes widened; he sat up straight, his attention fully on his cousin. "What? How?"

"His hand got infected and went putrid. The jailer called a surgeon, who amputated the arm, but either the poison had already hit his bloodstream or the procedure was somehow botched, because he was dead within a week." The colonel shook his head and frowned. "My man kept me informed, so I knew about the amputation, but I never thought it would end like this." He slapped his hand on the table. "Death was too easy for him. He has done too much damage to you and your family, and by extension mine, to get away so easily."

Darcy was quiet a long time, as were his companions. Then, he said, "I do not know how I feel about this. My thoughts are all over the place. It seems the apothecary in Meryton did not do a very good job when he treated the wound. Death, no matter how it happened, is a fitting revenge for all he has done. I feel badly that he is dead, and with few to mourn him. But mostly, when I think of him at all, I see Elizabeth struggling with him and I want to kill him myself." He shrugged and shook his head. "He will never be able to harm another of my loved ones, ever again."

"No, he will not," the earl stated. "I agree with my son that this was too easy a death for him."

Out of the corner of his eye, Darcy could

see his uncle watching him closely, but he kept his focus on the tumbler of port that sat in front of him.

Lord Matlock reached out and touched his nephew's arm. "Darcy, do not take on the blame for his death. It was not your doing, and if he had gone to trial, the end result would likely have been the same."

With a deep sigh, Darcy replied. "I know it is not. I just hate the thought that he might have died unrepentant."

"If he did, that is indeed a sad thing. But, we do not know it to be a fact, so I say none of us should dwell on it." The earl tilted his head, his gaze still pinned to his nephew. "You, for one, have a much more pleasant companion on whom to dwell." He laughed when Darcy grinned.

"I do." He mentally shook himself and then sat up straight. "And I intend to do so." He lifted his glass. "To Elizabeth Darcy." When his uncle and cousin lifted theirs, he tapped his to each and all three took a drink.

Later that night, after they had returned home and were snuggling in bed, Darcy told Elizabeth what he had learned from his cousin. She was silent for a long time, and eventually, Darcy could wait no longer for her response. "My love? Are you well?"

Elizabeth shifted, then looked up at him. "I am. I am trying to decide how I feel about it." She looked down and he could see her bite her lip.

Darcy caressed her arm. "What have you determined?"

She shrugged. "I feel bad that he died, as I would for anyone who did. However, he caused me a great deal of anxiety, and he would not have been injured had he not been trying to do me harm." She bit her lip again and looked up at him with a crease across her forehead. "Does that make me an evil person?"

Darcy shook his head, his hand not ceasing its movement up and down her limb. "No, it does not. You are correct about Wickham's injury. He did much harm to many people, not the least of which was Georgiana. That he was hurt in the process of attacking you is his own fault, and any result of that harm can also be laid at his door."

Elizabeth sighed. The crease in her brow deepened. "Will you tell your sister? Does she need to know?"

"I do not know the answer to either of those questions." Darcy kissed her hair. "I think for now, I will keep the information to myself. If she asks at a later date, I will tell her what happened. Or ..." He craned his neck to look at his wife's face where it rested on his shoulder. "You can, if she brings it up to you."

"I can do that. It is probably wise to let it rest for now. She may not care to know. It is not as though they have a continued connection. She may wish to completely forget him."

"I hope so." Darcy's fervent reply was accompanied by a squeeze to Elizabeth's shoulder, one she reciprocated by doing the same to his middle.

"Did Mr. Wickham give any statements before he died about his activities or his accomplices?"

Darcy shook his head. "Unfortunately, no. Of course, he was caught in the act of assaulting you, so that charge could not be disputed. He would have at least been deported for that. Fitzwilliam is disappointed that Wickham did not at least name the others involved in his scheme, though to be honest, depending on who he was involved with here in town, he may have been in danger to do so."

Elizabeth moved her head so she looked up at him again. "What do you mean?"

"Wickham, we assume, was taking the items stolen from homes by Mr. Denny and whomever else was involved in the thefts to London and selling them to someone else. There are leaders, if you will, of crime in the darkest portions of the city; men who essentially rule those neighborhoods with an iron fist. These criminal leaders are not afraid to kill anyone who crosses them. He may have feared for his life."

Elizabeth shuddered. She was silent for a few minutes, and Darcy began to wonder if she had fallen asleep. Suddenly, she spoke again.

"It fills me with dismay to know there are such people in the world." She sighed. "While

I am sorry Mr. Wickham has lost his life, his death was the result of his own actions. I cannot and do not regret injuring him. I do not wish to think of what would have happened to me had I not defended myself in such a manner." She looked up at Darcy, her jaw set. "I will think of it no more."

Darcy lifted his lips in a small smile as he caressed her cheek. "Then I will not, either." He kissed her. "I love you, Mrs. Darcy."

Elizabeth returned his smile. "I love you, as well, Mr. Darcy."

Epilogue

The season went on and Darcy and his new wife were invited to more soirees than they could possibly attend. Darcy had always hated socializing, so when Elizabeth suggested they choose only the most important ones to attend, he happily agreed. He was proud of his wife and glad to show her off, but it did not need to be all night, every night.

He was pleased to see Elizabeth adapting so well to her new society. Though not everyone liked her, she was able to charm most of the people she met with her quick wit and tendency toward impertinence. She was lively, and that drew people to her. Too, she was married to a powerful gentleman, if he did say so himself, and some, even those who disliked her, merely wished to remain on her good side. It mattered little to him what their reasons were, as long as they treated her with the respect she deserved.

It was now December. They had been married a month at this point, and no word had come to Elizabeth from Longbourn. She did not appear to mind the situation, so he did not mention it, until one Saturday when they were alone in the house's library.

Elizabeth was snuggled up to his side, an embroidery hoop in her hand, while Darcy had one arm around her and the other resting on the arm of the sofa, a book in its hand.

"Mary has had a letter from home."

Immediately, Darcy closed the book and turned his complete attention to his wife. "She has?"

Elizabeth nodded. "She has."

"Does this bother you?"

"Oh, no, not at all. It is rather a relief to me. I still get news of what is going on with my family but without the headache of being addressed directly and being forced to reply."

Darcy's brows rose. "I see. That makes sense. What did Mary's letter say?"

A slow grin spread over Elizabeth's face. "Jane is married."

"She found another gentleman to compromise?" Darcy felt sorry for the poor, unknown chap.

"Noooo." Elizabeth shook her head again. "She did not do the compromising."

Darcy's eyes widened. "What?"

Elizabeth giggled. "It seems that the Monday following our wedding, my father's cousin, who is to inherit and whom he has never met, arrived at Longbourn. Papa had known he was to visit for weeks but did not tell Mama until that very day. Kitty, who is the one who wrote to Mary, said that Mr. Collins is ridiculous. It seems he talks a great deal but makes little sense. For Kitty, who herself has little sense, to say that means that he must have been a true buffoon. She said Papa did little but laugh at him and push him into the company of his wife and daughters. She also said that our cousin smells bad and has greasy hair."

"Oh, my. What else did she say?"

"Well, he apparently came to 'extend an olive branch' to the daughters of the house, was quite put out to discover that one of them had married mere days before and taken her next sister to live with her, and immediately settled upon Jane as the companion of his future life. Mama did not like that and tried to steer him toward Kitty, since Mary was no longer a resident. However, it apparently did not take this Mr. Collins long to determine that the hinted-at suitor who was expected to ask for Jane's hand at any moment did not exist."

"Oh, my."

Elizabeth put down the embroidery she had been working on all this time. "The Gouldings at Haye Park held a ball on November twenty-sixth, and do you know what happened?"

Darcy fought a smile. He was greatly enjoying his wife's dramatic retelling of the story. "I do not. Will you tell me?"

"Mr. Collins had asked each of my sisters for a set of dances. He insisted on dancing with Jane first. So they lined up and went through the set, and then disappeared. Halfway through the next set, a scream was heard above the music. All eyes turned toward the back of the room. There, through the open French doors to the balcony, could be seen my sister Jane and Mr. Collins in a compromising position. Mama fainted and Papa became angry, but they were married once the banns had been called. That was last week." Elizabeth wore a smile that could only be described as satisfied.

"Well." Darcy smiled at the thought of the mean-spirited Jane married to a man she did not like. "That will make an interesting marriage, do you not think?"

"Oh it will!" Elizabeth nodded vigorously. "Kitty told Mary that Jane cried and screamed and threw a tantrum but that Papa would not relent."

"I do not blame him, to be honest."

"Nor I," Elizabeth replied. "There is more."

"There is?"

"Yes." Elizabeth bit her lip. "You remember the aunt you told me about who objected to our marriage?"

"Lady Catherine?" Darcy's brows drew together.

"What was her surname?"

"DeBourgh."

Elizabeth lifted her chin. "I thought so. Well, Mr. Collins was recently ordained. He was appointed the rector of the church at Hunsford, which abuts Rosings Park-"

"My aunt's estate." Darcy threw his head back to rest against the sofa. "Good heavens. I remember her saying something in a letter back at Easter about getting a new clergyman. At the time, I was engaged in hiring a companion for my sister and paid little attention to the matter."

"Have you heard from her?"

He lifted his head to look at his wife. "No, not since I announced our marriage. She has not forgiven me for not marrying her daughter."

"Poor Darcy, hunted like an animal." Elizabeth's tease was accompanied by a kiss to his chin.

He rolled his eyes and then sniffed. "Poor Darcy indeed." He grinned at her laugh, and then kissed her, which led to him locking the door and showing his wife just how much he appreciated her and her teases.

Later, as they cuddled in front of the fire under a blanket, Elizabeth surprised him with a question.

"Will we have to see Jane and Mr. Collins often, with him being your aunt's rector?"

Darcy remained quiet for a while as he considered her inquiry. Eventually, he said, "Not necessarily and only if my aunt decides to leave off her complaints and to reconcile with me. We will not visit unless and until she does, and I doubt the Collinses will have the funds for frequent travel to either London or Derbyshire."

"True." Elizabeth's reply was a murmur and it was clear to her husband that she was thinking the situation over. "And since you and I have no desire to return to Longbourn, there will be no chance of being forced into their company there, either." She sighed. "It is probably not a good feeling to have, but I am glad. I do not need someone like Jane in my life." She moved her head, which was resting on Darcy's chest, so she could see his face. "I have much better sisters here, with you."

Darcy smiled, caressing her bare arm with his hand. "Speaking of sisters, how are things going with Mary and Fitzwilliam?"

"I think she is only waiting for him to ask the question. From what I can gather, she is eager for him to do so."

"They appear to be quite enamored of each other." Darcy smiled. "They are besotted."

Elizabeth giggled. "They are. I hope that when they do decide to marry, they do not wait as long as Miss Bingley is to hold the ceremony. Three months is a long time to be preparing for something that lasts an hour, at most."

Darcy chuckled. "I agree, but I suspect our impatience with it stems from our own speedy nuptials."

"Maybe. We did marry far more quickly than most." Elizabeth squeezed his middle. "But I am happy we did. I cannot imagine having to wait to experience all that you have shown me."

"If we had spent our betrothal period in town, I would have taken you to the museums and theater then, but we did not."

"I will grant you that. It would have made waiting that long so much easier. Still, I am happy with the way things went, at least as far as our betrothal and marriage. There were other aspects to that fortnight I could have done without," she added dryly.

Darcy snorted. "I agree." He fell into silence, almost drifting off to sleep until Elizabeth spoke again.

"About the letter Mary received ... there was another bit to it that I wished to share with you," she added, licking her lips with a suddenly uneasy appearance.

"What is it?" Darcy's brow creased at her apparent discomfort.

"She said that Mr. Denny was arrested and is facing a court martial. It seems an officer or officers from the regulars conducted an investigation into illegal activities within the militia unit."

"Really?" Darcy was intrigued. "Did she say anything else about it?"

"Kitty did not in her letter, but Mary told me that your cousin has been working on some sort of secret investigation ever since we left Meryton. He has not told her much, but she has gathered from hints he has dropped that it involved something there. Perhaps this is what it was?"

"Could be. I know he was very much disturbed to hear Wickham had died without giving up what he knew. It would be just like my cousin to persuade his superiors to allow him to scrutinize the situation. The militia and the regulars are two different entities, but Fitzwilliam dislikes anyone making soldiers appear as less than honorable."

"He is a good man." Elizabeth smiled up at Darcy. "Just like you."

"Thank you, my love." Darcy kissed her upturned lips.

"I liked the lady Mr. Bingley escorted to the ball last night. She is quiet but has a true serenity about her. She is not merely displaying a peaceful front as Jane does. She truly just exudes peace. It is almost contagious."

"She was delightful, I agree, and he seemed quite taken with her."

"As did she," Elizabeth was quick to point out. "Did you not see her countenance light up every time he looked her way?"

"I confess I did not notice. I was more taken by the fact that she looks so much like your sister, all blonde hair, blue eyes, and thin figure; though, the more I think on it, the more I realize that he has always liked blondes above all women." He looked down at his wife's upturned face and smirked. "I clearly prefer curvy brunettes." He winked.

Elizabeth laughed, her eyes twinkling in the way he loved so much. "Clearly." She snuggled back down into him. "Perhaps there will be a third wedding to attend in the next year."

The clock on the mantel soon chimed the

hour and the couple reluctantly rose and dressed, prepared to behave themselves in front of their sisters. As they exited the library, Mary came rushing down the hall, a look of excitement like nothing Darcy thought she was capable of transforming her countenance.

"Mary, what is it?" Elizabeth let go of her husband's arm to grasp her sister's hands.

"Oh, Lizzy, I am so happy! Is it good to be so? I am not gloating, am I? But still, to finally have something I have yearned for and waited so patiently for ..."

"What are you talking about?" Elizabeth laughed. "I must know so that I can be happy with you!"

"He has asked me to marry him and I said yes!" Mary suddenly met Darcy's eyes. "Oh, Brother ... he has gone to find you." She spun around.

"Do not fret; he will probably come here when he does not find me in my study. Look, there he is." Darcy could hardly wait to tease the colonel about his upcoming wedding. After he gave his permission, of course.

Once he had teased Fitzwilliam and made him beg for Mary's hand, he offered his cousin a glass of port.

"Yes, thank you. I could use one after that inquisition." The colonel pulled a handkerchief out of his pocket and wiped his brow.

Darcy laughed. "Oh, come now. It was not that bad."

Fitzwilliam snorted. "I am sure it was not from your perspective." He accepted the tumbler of red liquid and took a sip.

Darcy settled into his chair once more, glass in hand. "What is your next step?"

"You mean other than visiting my solicitor and preparing Mary's settlement?" At Darcy's nod, the colonel continued. "I will resign my commission, or try to. I may need to wait until Napoleon is finally conquered. The army is in need of officers and even though I was injured too badly to continue fighting in that last campaign, new recruits are still in need of training and there are too few of us to fill the need."

Darcy looked solemnly at his friend. "So it is a settled thing that you will not be sent back to the fighting?"

Fitzwilliam nodded. "Yes, it is. I cannot sit astride like I used to be able to. More than an hour in the saddle at a time leaves me nearly immobile. My superiors have seen this and have assured me I am home for the duration."

Darcy did not know what to say. He looked into his glass for a long moment. Finally, he said, "I am glad." He looked up. "We will not have to worry about you so much."

The colonel lifted a corner of his lips in a brief grin. "Until I resign, we will have to live here in town, Mary and I. However, I have that estate my uncle left me. At some point in the future, I wish to live there. Mary assures me that where ever I go, she wants to be with me, and though I would not allow her to follow me to war, I am happy that she does not require me to give up either the estate or town like one of those brainless debutantes my mother was thrusting at me would have."

Darcy chuckled. "I understand your position. I do not think they are all brainless, but certainly, many are."

Fitzwilliam shook his head and changed the subject. "Mother was thrilled when I told her I was ready to propose. She has come to love Mary as much as I do."

"She is a delightful young lady under all that seriousness. She has blossomed during your courtship." Darcy smiled and raised a brow. "Elizabeth and I were remarking on that last night."

"She had it in her all the time. She just ..." The colonel blushed.

"She needed you to bring it out of her." Darcy chuckled at the grin taking over his cousin's face, but then turned the conversation to something else. "Elizabeth tells me Mary got a letter from Longbourn today."

Fitzwilliam scowled. "I hope it was not from her mother."

"No, it was from Miss Catherine." Darcy tilted his head. "It mentioned one of the officers and an investigation that was done into the activities of certain militia members."

A slow smile began to overtake the colonel's features, but he leaned back in his chair and sipped his drink. "Did she now?"

Darcy nodded, examining his grinning cousin with a sharp eye. "I take it you were involved somehow?"

"I was. Did this letter mention which officer was investigated?"

"Mr. Denny."

Fitzwilliam chortled. "Ah, yes, Mr. Denny. I suppose you would like to know what happened and what my involvement was."

Darcy lifted and lowered his shoulders. "I confess I would, if you can tell me."

"It is all over now, so I can, though I would ask you not to share with anyone other than Elizabeth."

Darcy nodded. "You have my word."

"Mr. Denny and another officer, a corporal named Saunders, were working with Wickham to steal from houses in the Meryton area. They had done the same in other places the unit had been stationed in. Denny and Saunders, when confronted, quickly gave up details. Their commanding officer, Colonel Forster, was beside himself with anger. He declared that though he could not officially court-martial them, he could and would hold a tribunal. He gathered together a dozen officers he trusted, called for the accused to stand before them and interrogated them for hours. In the end, the verdict was guilty as charged. Forster would have had them executed right then and there, but the twelve insisted he hold the guilty men to be tried at the assizes at Epiphany. However ..." Fitzwilliam paused, seemingly attempting to draw out the drama. "It appears Denny and Saunders were afraid of the punishment they would face and tried to flee in the night. They wcrc shot by soldiers set as pickets just past the edge of the encampment."

Darcy could feel a slow smile spreading over his face. "A fitting end, I would say. Elizabeth will be pleased."

And she was.

~ ~ ~***~ ~ ~

That night, after a dinner celebrating the engagement of Colonel Fitzwilliam to Mary Bennet, Darcy and Elizabeth retired to their bedchamber. They crawled into their bed, holding each other and talking, much like they had earlier in the library. Eventually, the events of the day caught up with them and they drifted off to sleep. The last thing Darcy remembered thinking was how happy he was to have compromised his Elizabeth.

The End

Before you go ...

If you enjoyed this book, please consider leaving a review at the store where you purchased it.

Also, consider joining my mailing list at

https://mailchi.mp/ee42ccbc6409/zoeburton signup

~Zoe

About the Author

Zoe Burton first fell in love with Jane Austen's books in 2010, after seeing the 2005 version of Pride and Prejudice on television. While making her purchases of Miss Austen's novels, she discovered Jane Austen Fan Fiction; soon after that she found websites full of JAFF. Her life has never been the same. She began writing her own stories when she ran out of new ones to read.

Zoe lives in a 100-plus-year-old house in the snow-belt of Ohio with her Boxer, Jasper. She is a former Special Education Teacher, and has a passion for romance in general, *Pride and Prejudice* in particular, and stock car racing.

Connect with Zoe Burton

Email:
zoe@zoeburton.com

Facebook:
https://www.facebook.com/ZoeBurtonBooks
https://www.facebook.com/groups/BurtonsBabes/

Pinterest:
https://www.pinterest.com/zoeburtonauthor/

Website:
https://zoeburton.com

Join my mailing list:
https://mailchi.mp/ee42ccbc6409/zoeburtonsignup

Support me at Patreon:
https://www.patreon.com/zoeburtonauthor

Me at Austen Authors:
http://austenauthors.net/zoe-burton/

Darcy's Christmas Compromise

Darcy's Predicament

Darcy's Uneasy Betrothal

Darcy's Yuletide Wedding

Darcy's Unwanted Bride

Darcy's Favorite

Darcy's Christmas Scheme

Darcy's Christmas Ball

Mr. Darcy: The Key to Her Heart

Victorian Romance:

A MUCH Later Meeting

WESTERN ROMANCE:

Darcy's Bodie Mine

Bundles:

Darcy's Adventures

Forced to Wed

Promises

Mr. Darcy Finds Love (available exclusively to
newsletter subscribers)

The Darcy Marriage Series Books 1-3

Mr. Darcy, My Hero

Coming Together

Christmas in Meryton

The Darcy Marriage Series:

Darcy's Wife Search

Lady Catherine Impedes

Caroline's Censure

Pride & Prejudice & Racecars

Darcy's Race to Love

Georgie's Redemption

Darcy's Caution

Made in the USA
Coppell, TX
05 December 2022

87912480R00114